THE PRINCESS DIARIES 2
ROYAL ENGAGEMENT

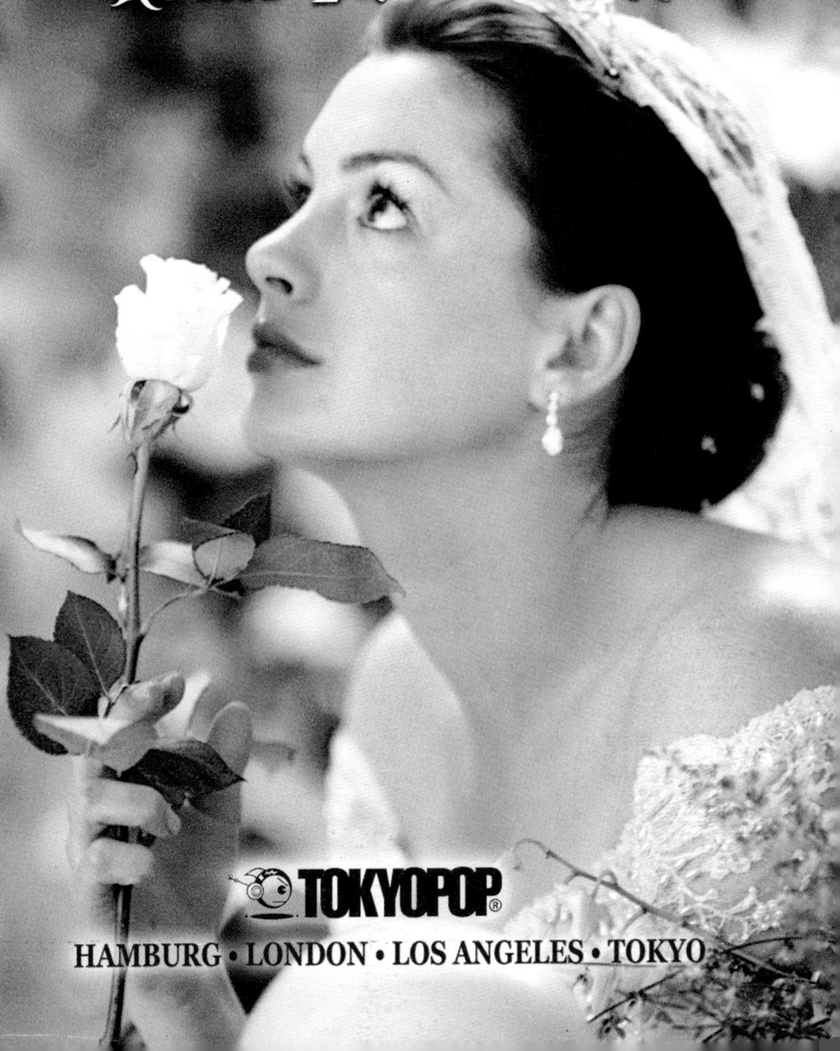

TOKYOPOP®

HAMBURG • LONDON • LOS ANGELES • TOKYO

Editor - Erin Stein
Photography Editor - Sarah Hadley
Graphic Designer and Letterer - Monalisa J. de Asis
Cover Designer - Anna Kernbaum
Graphic Artist - Michael Paolilli

Digital Imaging Manager - Chris Buford
Pre-Press Manager - Antonio DePietro
Production Managers - Jennifer Miller and Mutsumi Miyazaki
Senior Designer - Suzanna Lakatos
Art Director - Matt Alford
Senior Editor - Elizabeth Hurchalla
Managing Editor - Jill Freshney
Editor in Chief - Mike Kiley
VP of Production - Ron Klamert
President & C.O.O. - John Parker
Publisher & C.E.O. - Stuart Levy

E-mail: info@tokyopop.com
Come visit us online at www.TOKYOPOP.com

A TOKYOPOP® Cine-Manga® Book
TOKYOPOP Inc.
5900 Wilshire Blvd., Suite 2000
Los Angeles, CA 90036

The Princess Diaries 2: Royal Engagement

ISBN: 1-59532-086-5

First TOKYOPOP® printing: February 2005

10 9 8 7 6 5 4 3 2 1

Printed in the USA

THE PRINCESS DIARIES 2
ROYAL ENGAGEMENT

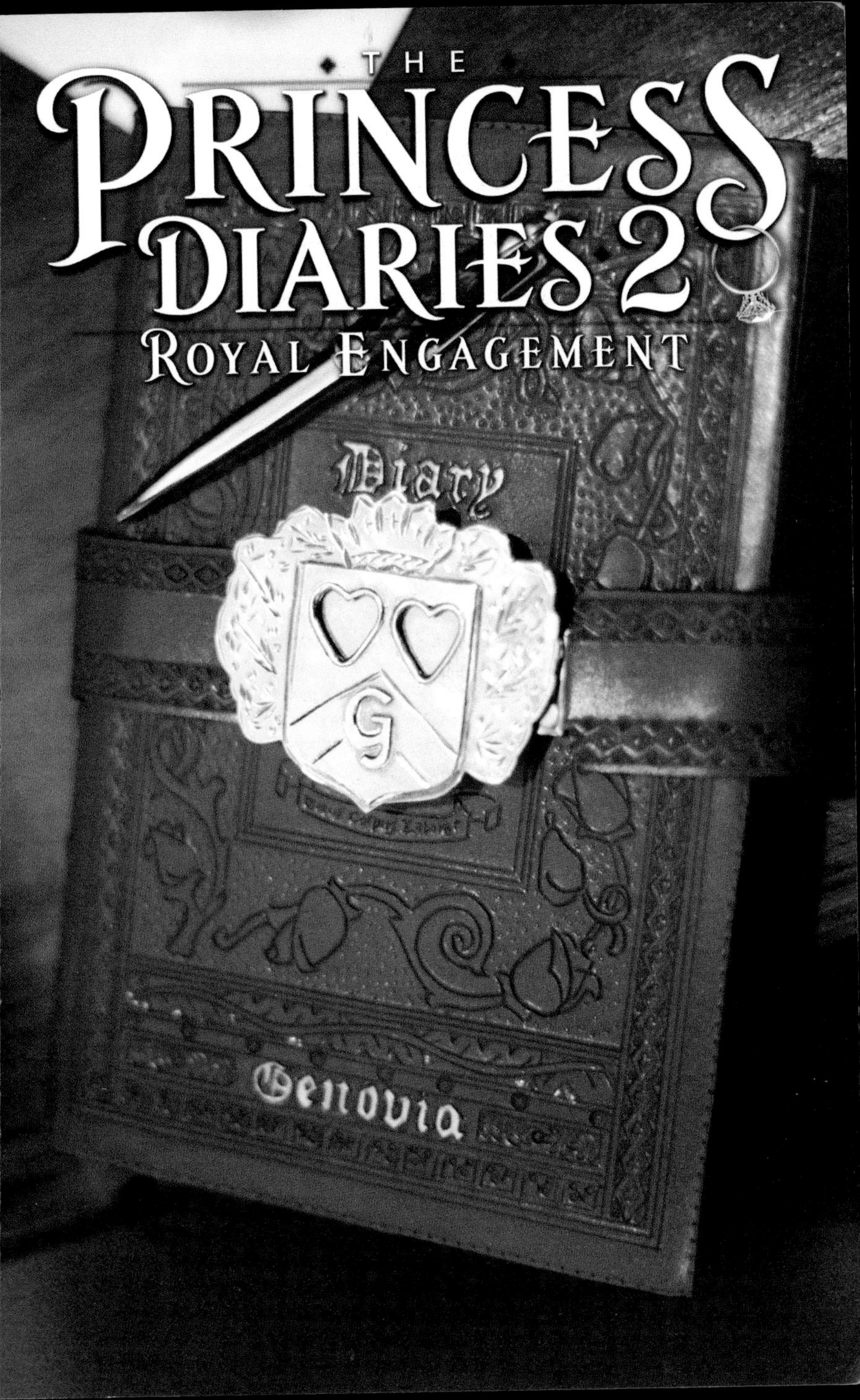
Diary
G
Genovia

Who's Who in Genovia

Let's meet the
royal family and
those closest to the
inner circle.

Her Royal Highness
Queen Clarisse Renaldi.
Genovia's beloved queen has
ruled as regent since the death
of her son, King Phillipe,
who was Mia's father.

Her Royal Highness
Princess Amelia Mignonette
Thermopolis Renaldi. Genovia
found its princess in a high school
in San Francisco! She came home
after college to take over the
throne as queen.

The completely eligible Andrew Jacoby, Duke of Kenilworth.

Lord Nicholas Devereaux,
a dashing young man!
He is Princess Mia's rival
for the throne.

The mysterious
Joseph is head of security
for the palace and utterly
devoted to the queen.

Viscount Arthur Mabrey
is a member of Parliament
and Nicholas Devereaux's uncle.
He wants his nephew
to become king.

Lilly Moscovitz is
Princess Mia's best friend.
Lilly spent the summer
in lovely Genovia at
the palace.

The queen's
canine companion,
Maurice, has always been
Genovia's top dog.

Princess Mia's cat,
Fat Louie, now lives in
the lap of luxury
at the palace.

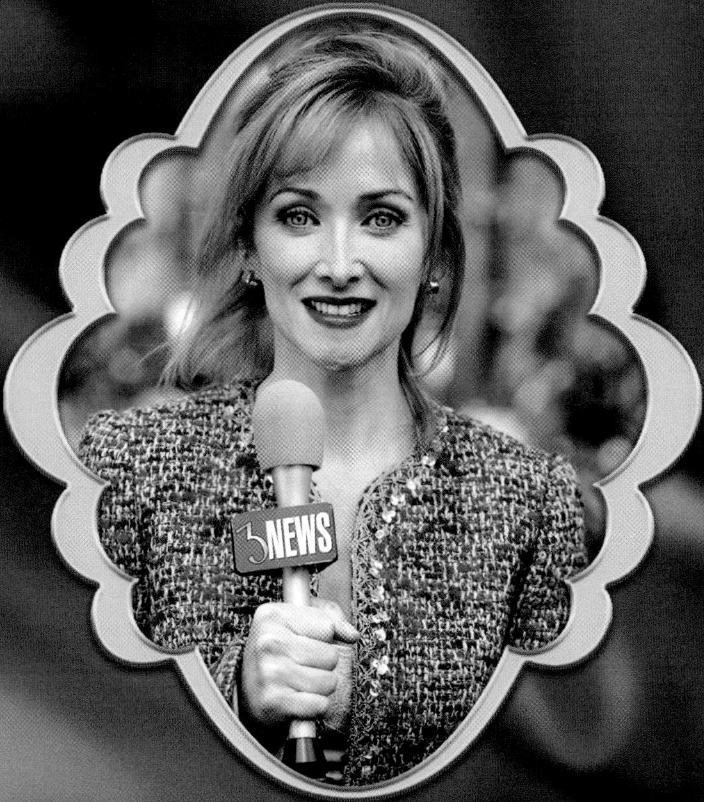
3NEWS

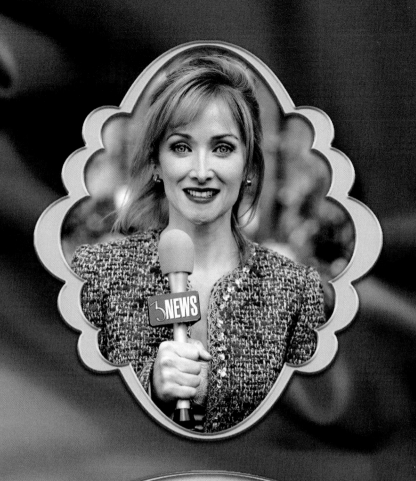

And I'm Elsie Kentworthy,
your Palace Insider.
Let's find out what our
princess has been up to
this year, shall we?

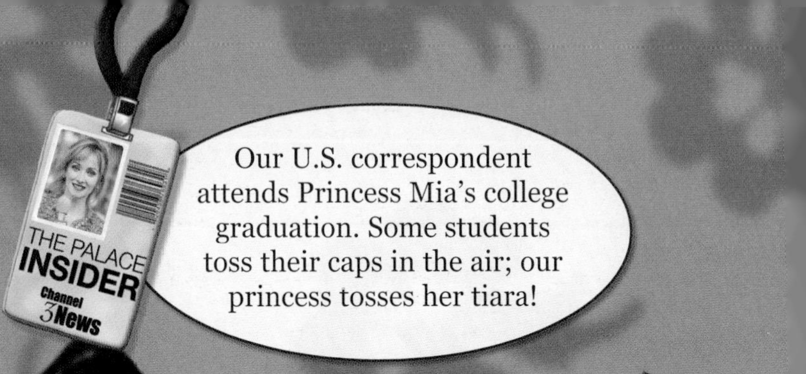
THE PALACE
INSIDER
Channel
3 News

Our U.S. correspondent attends Princess Mia's college graduation. Some students toss their caps in the air; our princess tosses her tiara!

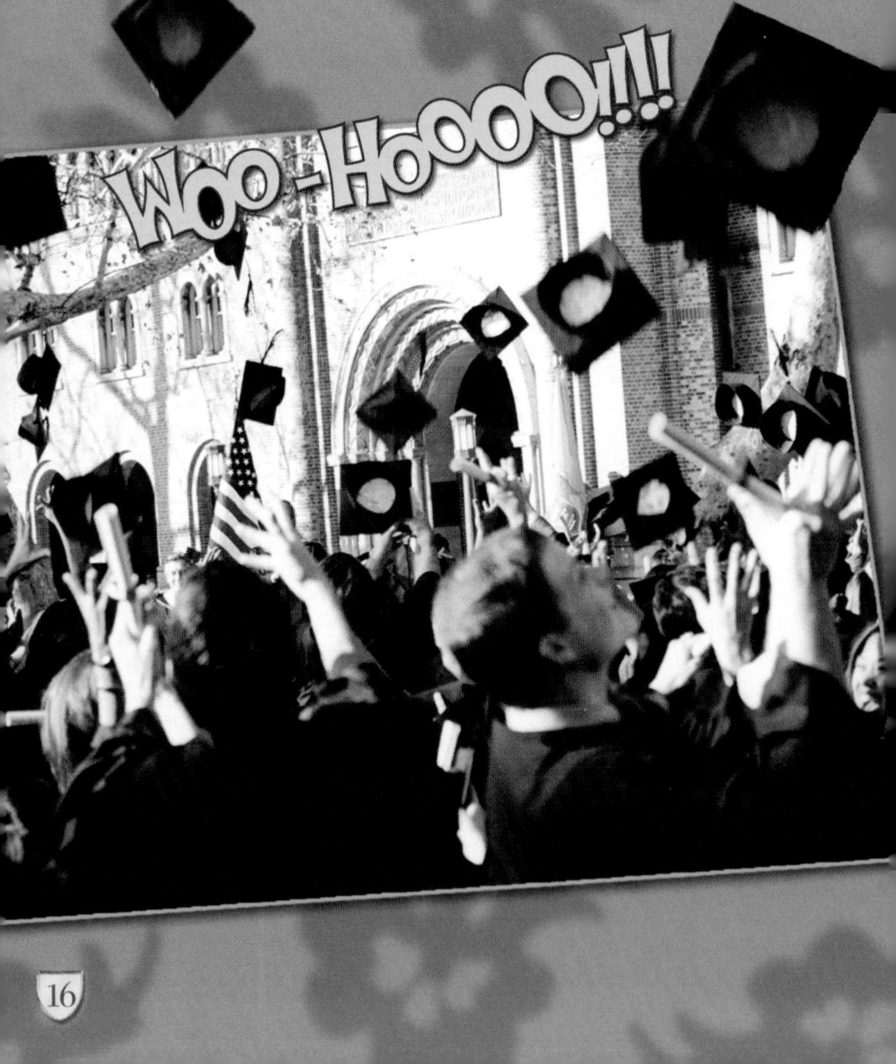
WOO-HOOOO!!!

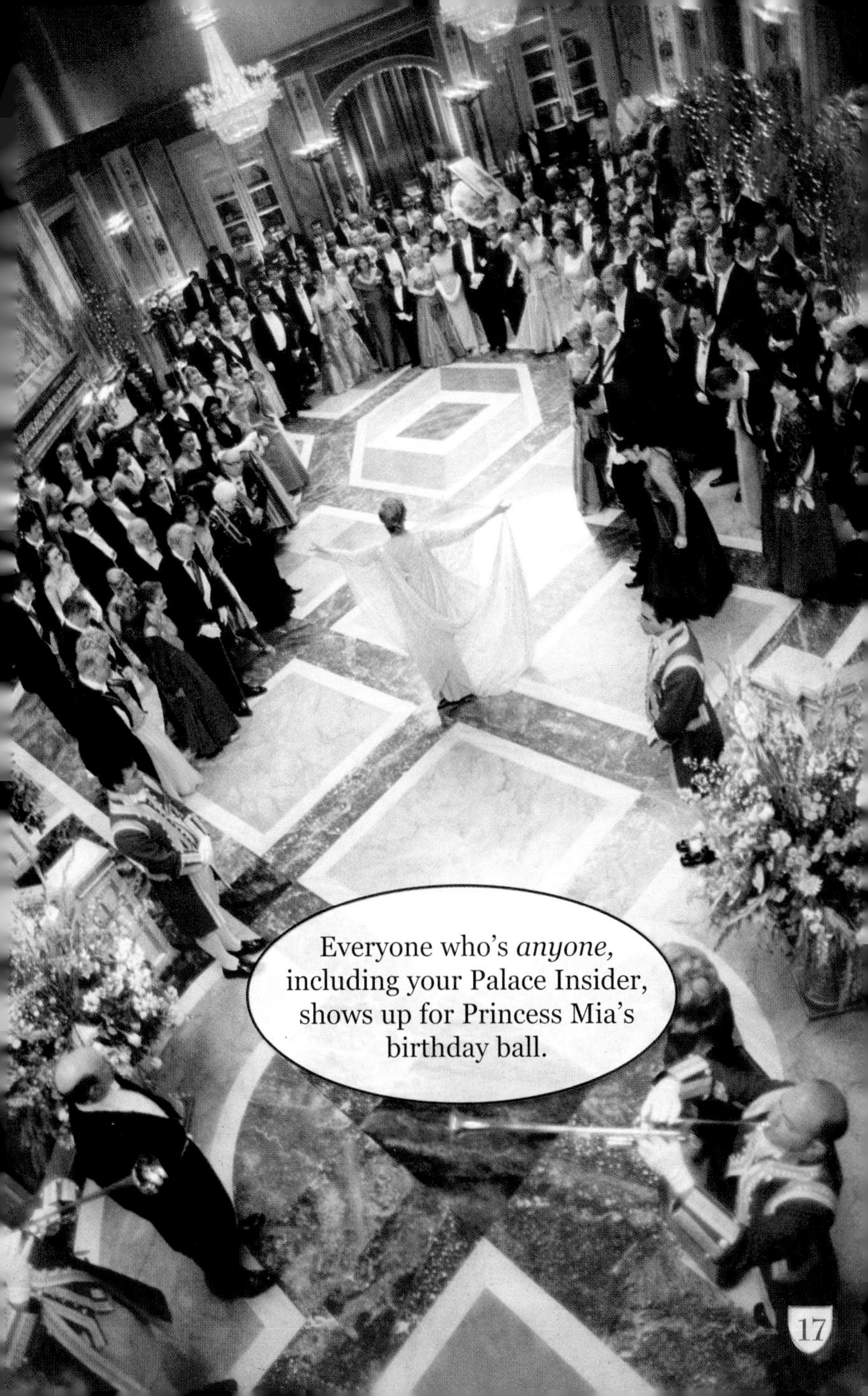

Everyone who's *anyone*, including your Palace Insider, shows up for Princess Mia's birthday ball.

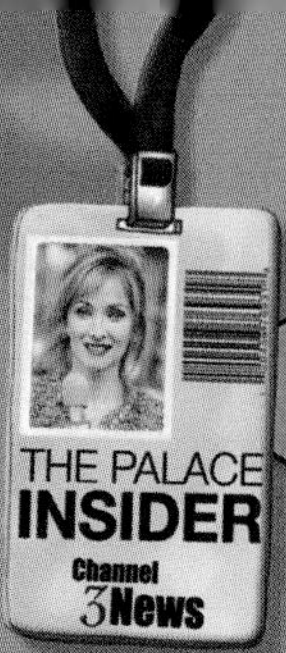
THE PALACE
INSIDER
Channel
3News

The princess dances with all of Genovia's eligible bachelors.

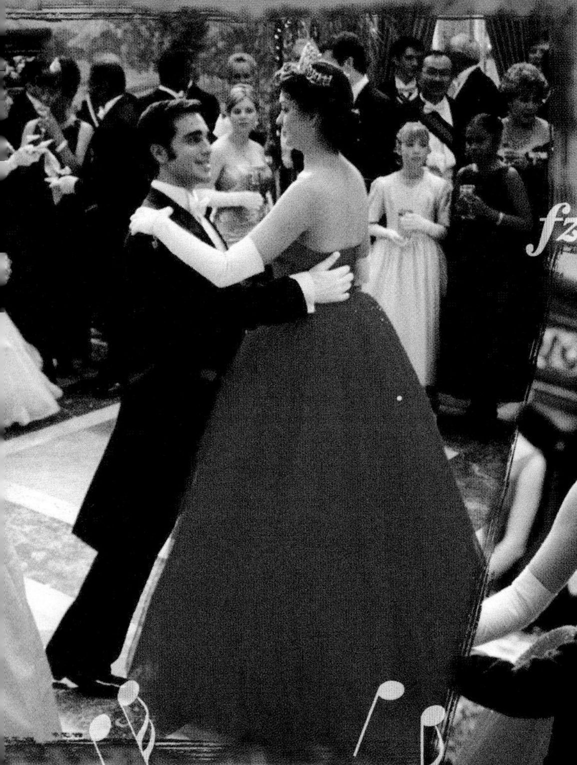

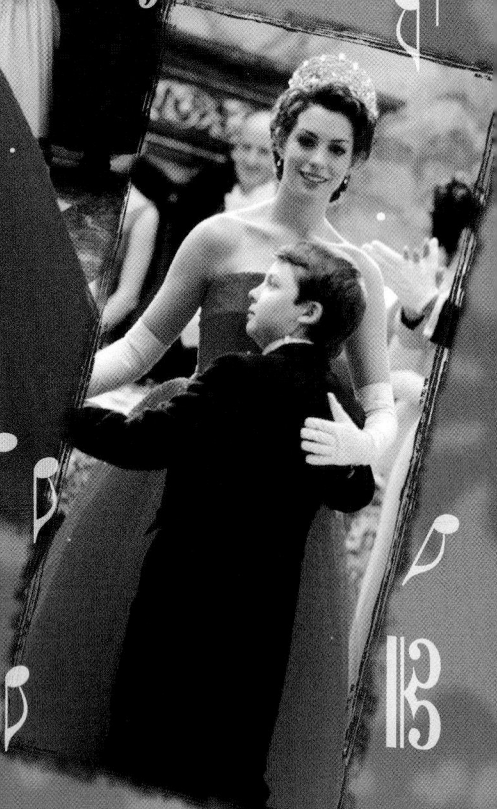

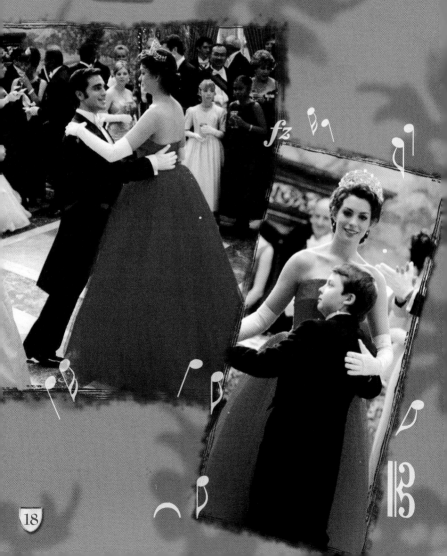

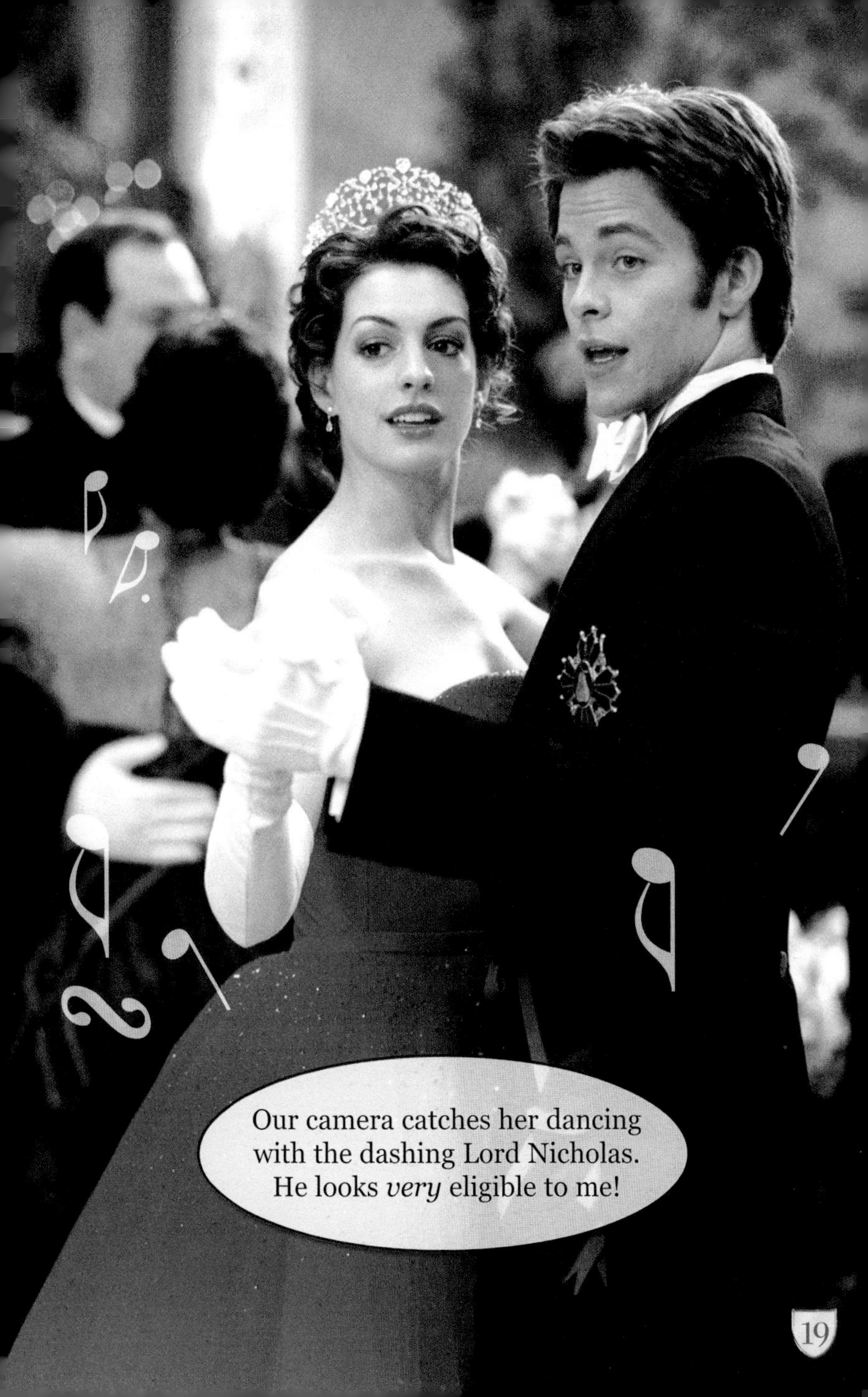

Our camera catches her dancing
with the dashing Lord Nicholas.
He looks *very* eligible to me!

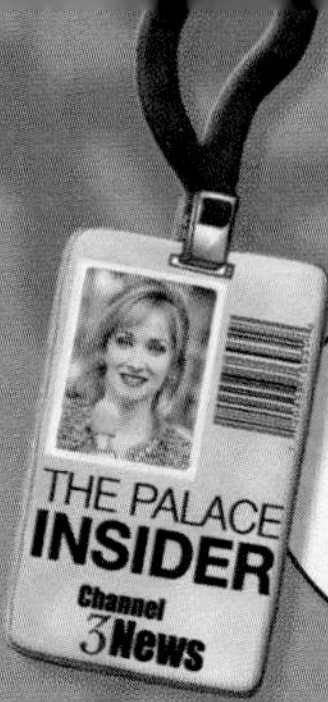
THE PALACE
INSIDER
Channel
3News

Time to learn how to be a queen! Daily queen lessons, then a meeting with Genovians in the throne room. Being a princess is not a piece of Genovian cake.

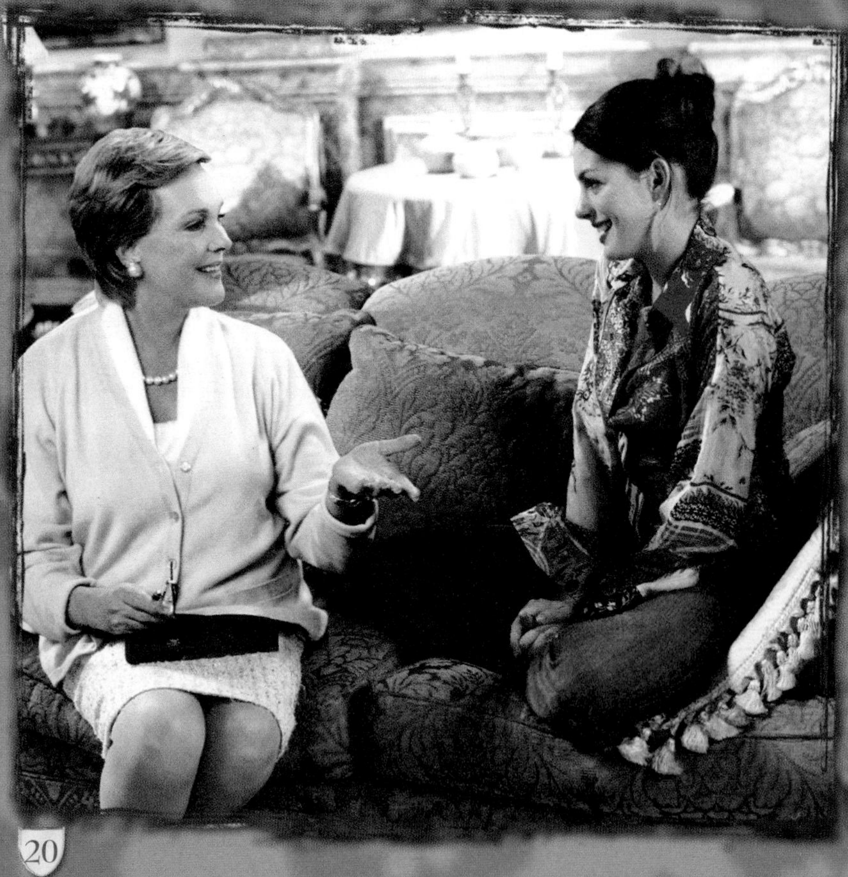

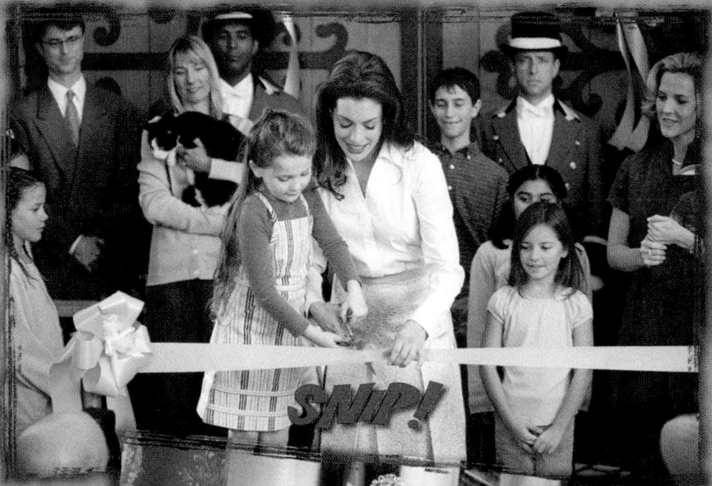
SNIP!

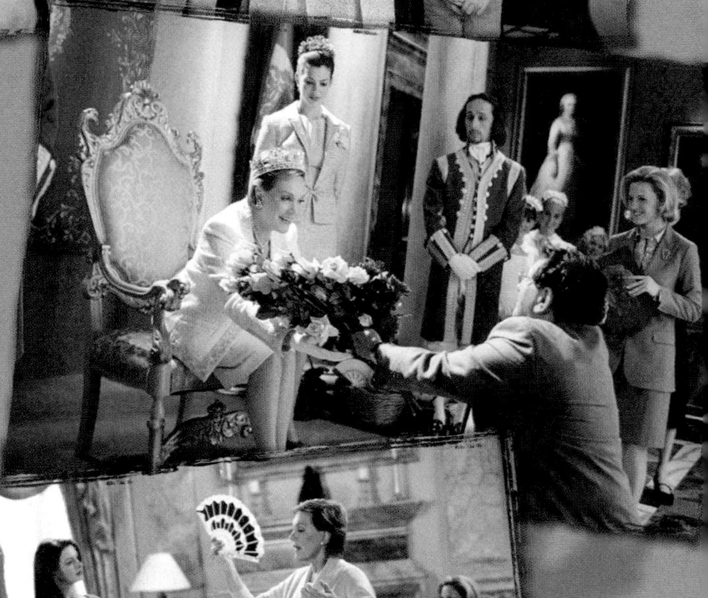

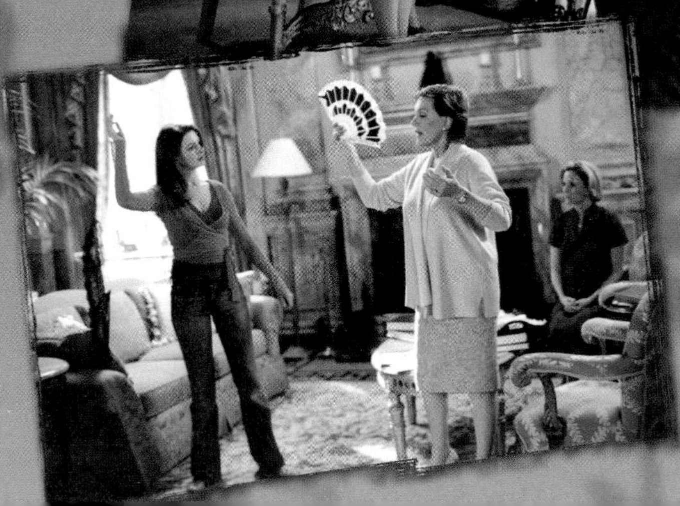

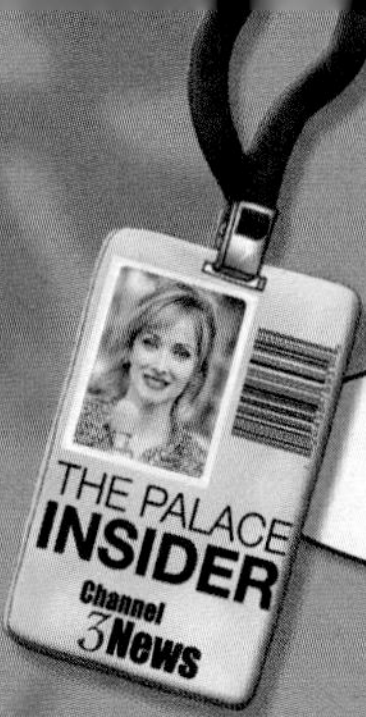
THE PALACE
INSIDER
Channel
3News

Princess Mia meets
with Parliament.

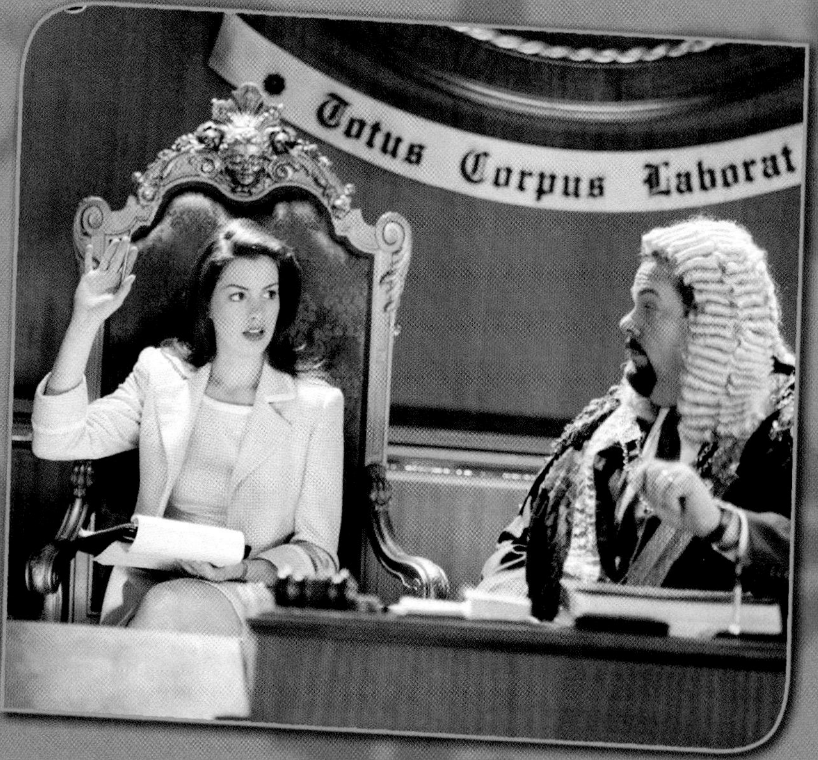
Totus Corpus Laborat

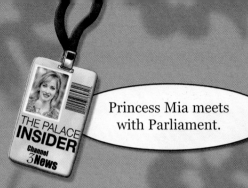

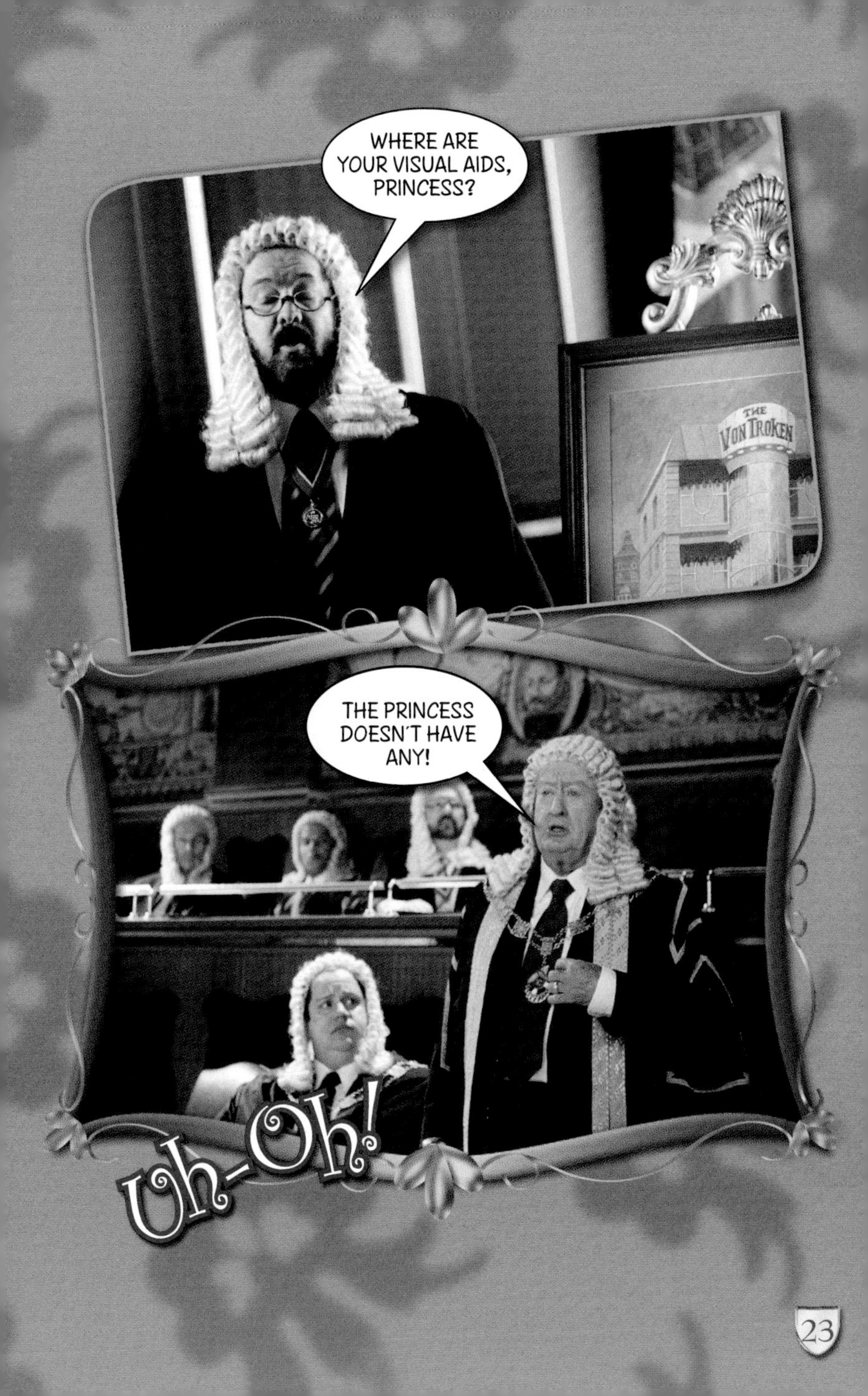
WHERE ARE YOUR VISUAL AIDS, PRINCESS?
THE PRINCESS DOESN'T HAVE ANY!
THE VON TROKEN
Uh-Oh!

THE PALACE INSIDER
Channel 3 News

Let's see how the princess adjusts to her other royal duties. Is she calm or clumsy as she inspects the Genovian Royal Guard?

CLIP-CLOP!

CLIP-CLOP!

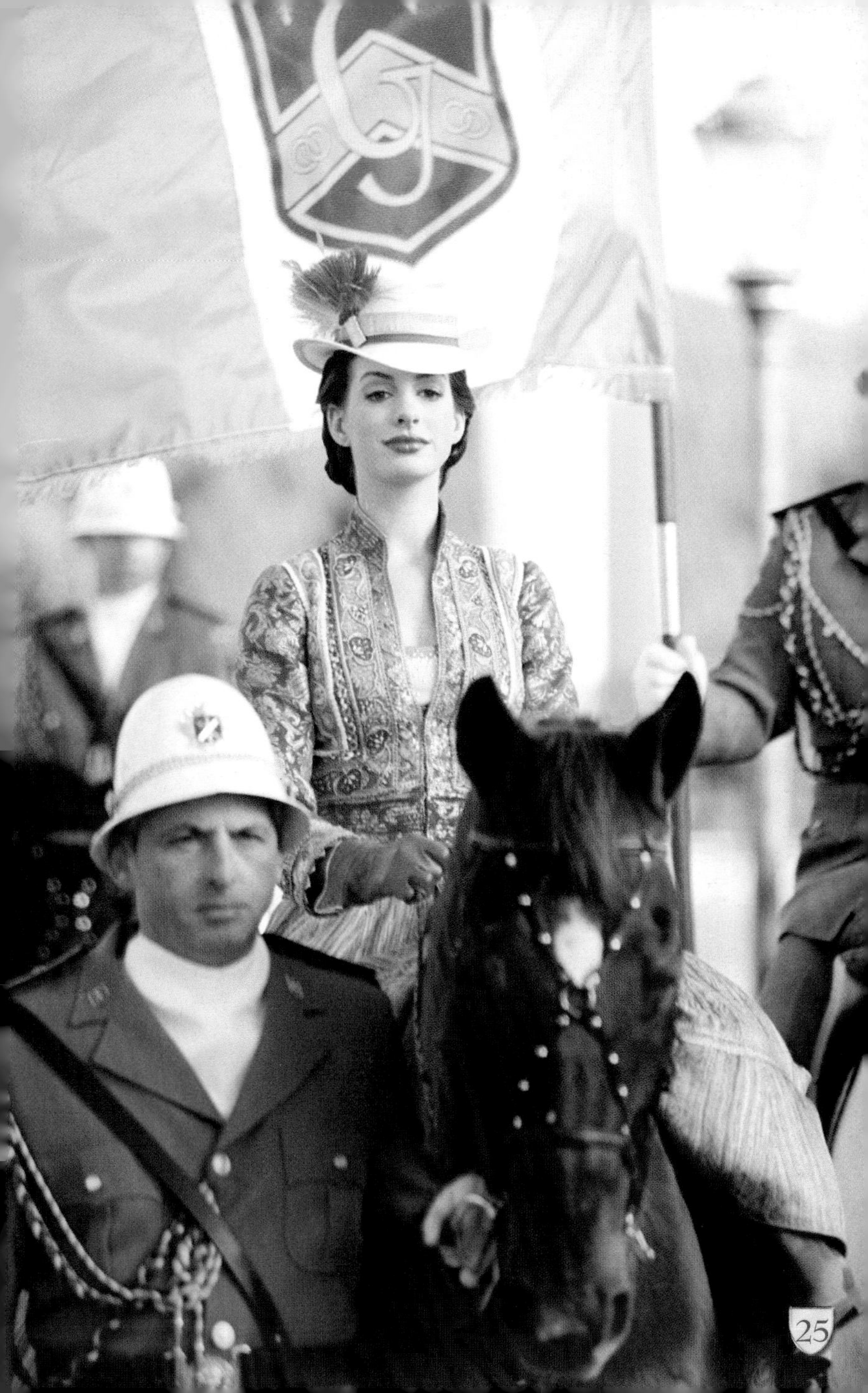

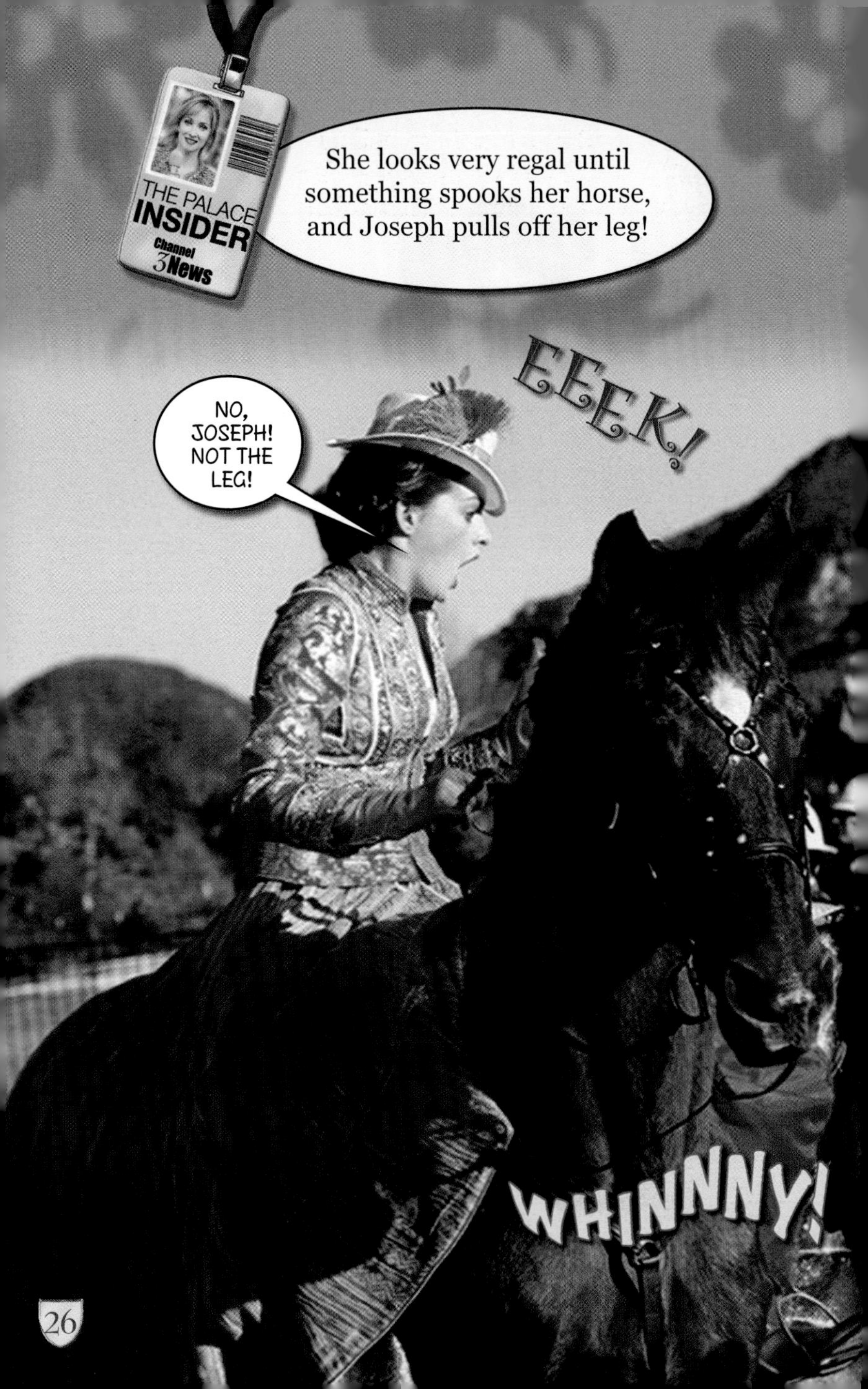
THE PALACE INSIDER
Channel 3News
She looks very regal until something spooks her horse, and Joseph pulls off her leg!
EEEK!
NO, JOSEPH! NOT THE LEG!
WHINNNY!

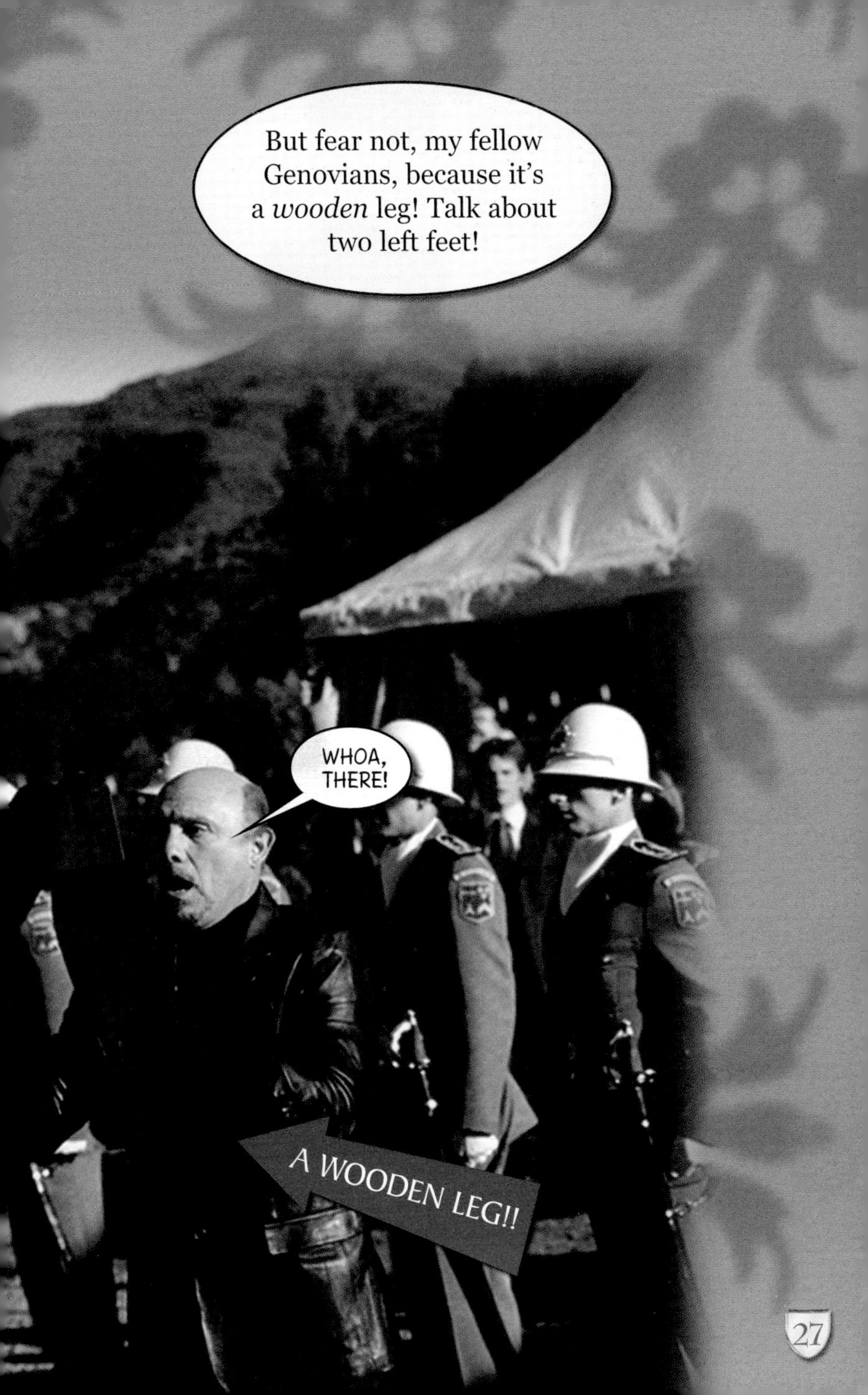
But fear not, my fellow Genovians, because it's a *wooden* leg! Talk about two left feet!
WHOA, THERE!
A WOODEN LEG!!

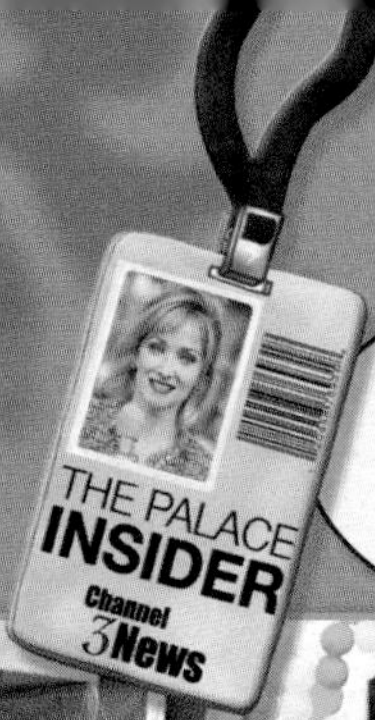
THE PALACE
INSIDER
Channel
3News

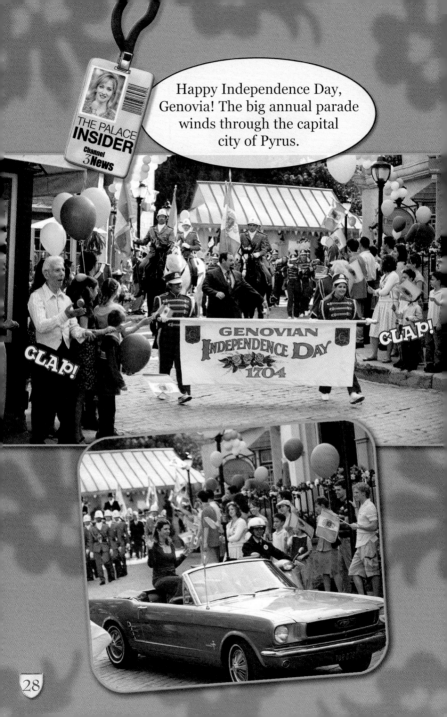

Happy Independence Day, Genovia! The big annual parade winds through the capital city of Pyrus.

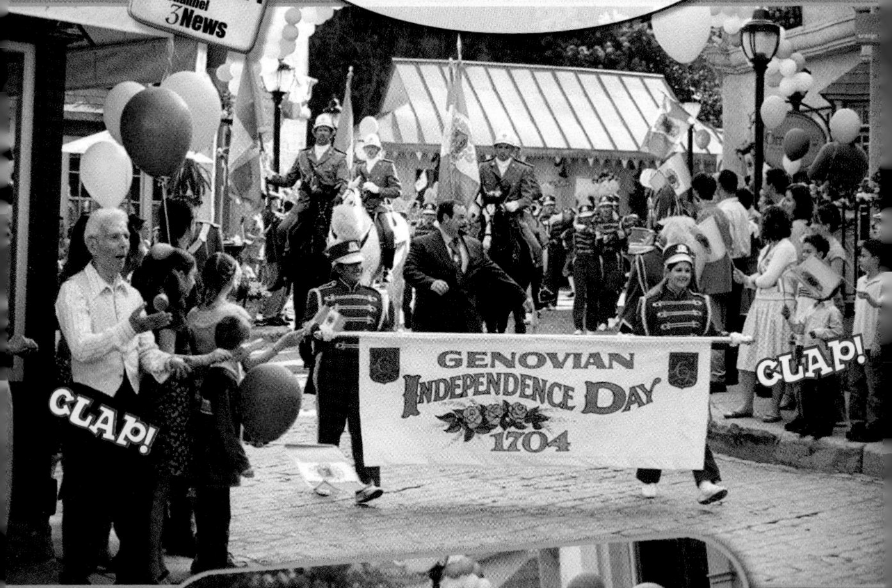
GENOVIAN
INDEPENDENCE DAY
1704
CLAP!
CLAP!

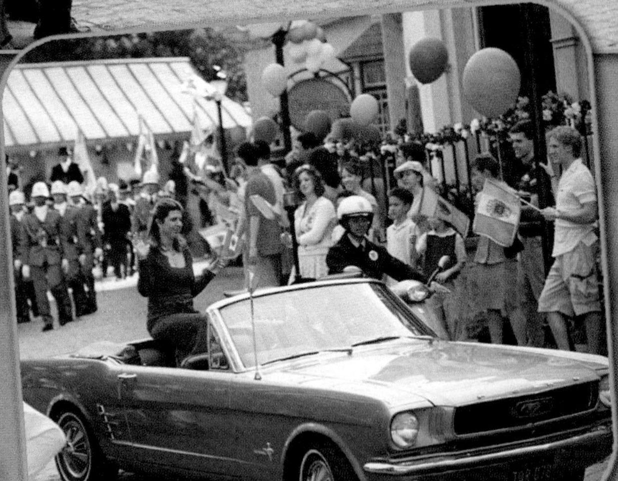

Our princess and
queen look spectacular in
all those jewels!

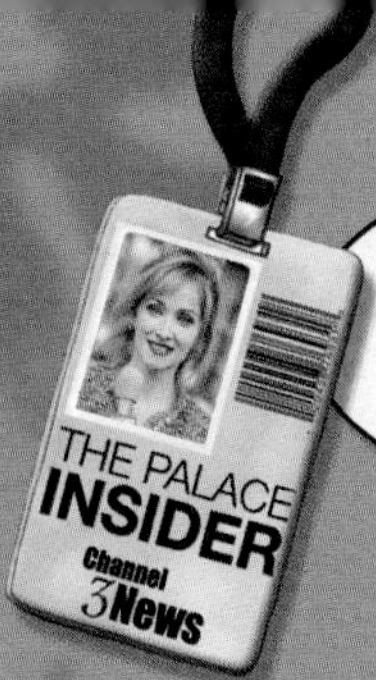
THE PALACE
INSIDER
Channel
3News

Would you look at this?
Princess Mia is leaving
the parade.

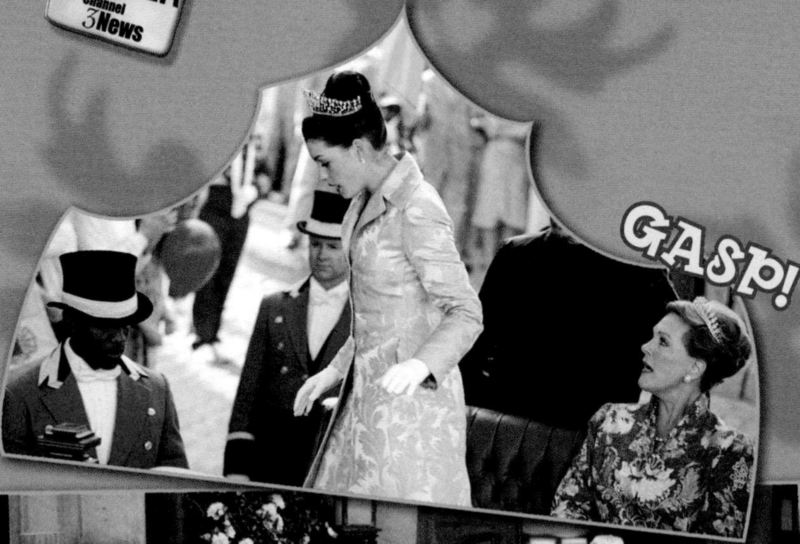
GASP!

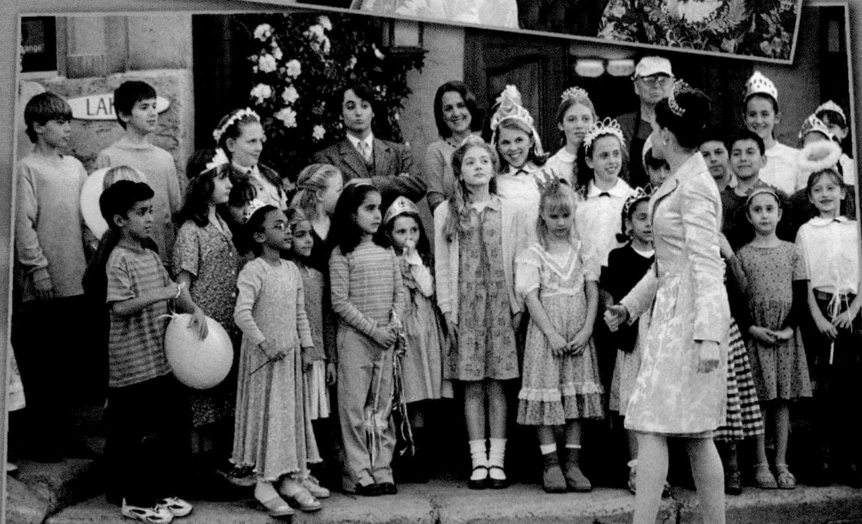

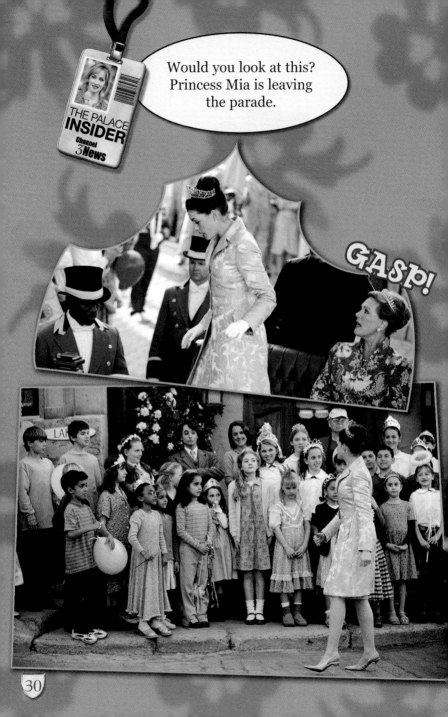

HOORAY!

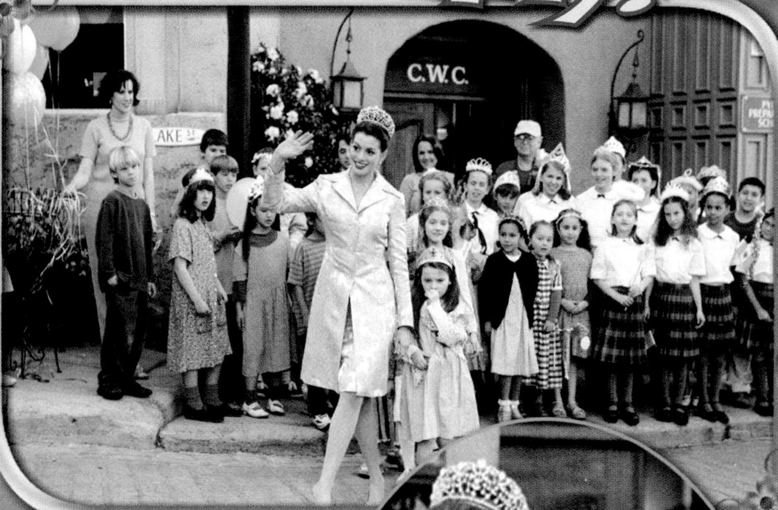
C.W.C.

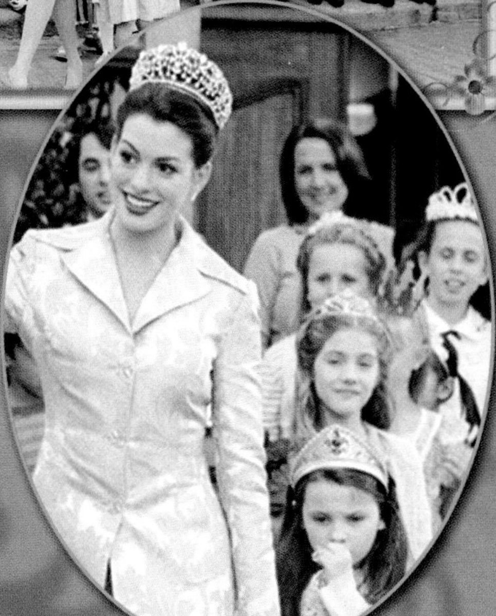

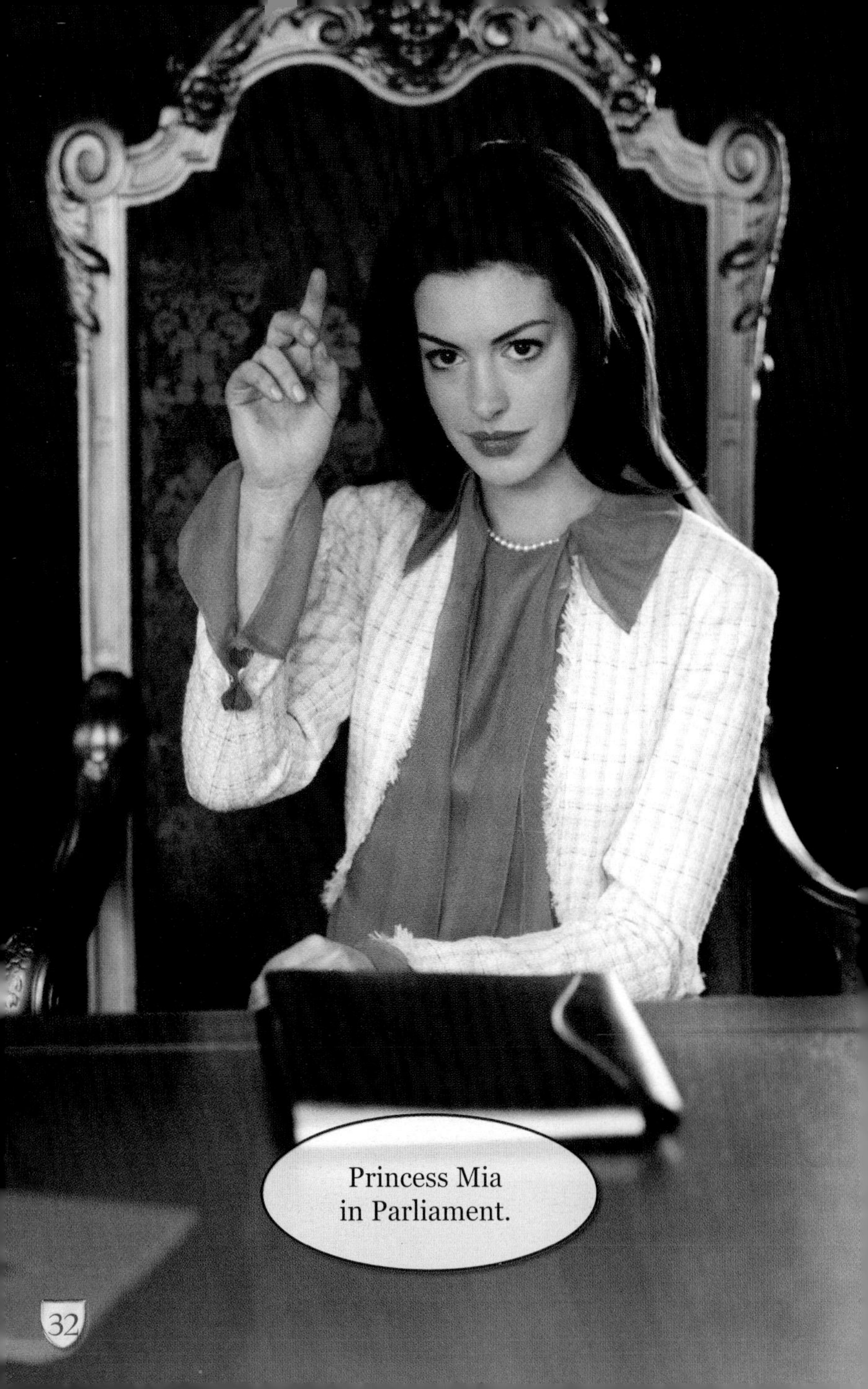

Princess Mia
in Parliament.

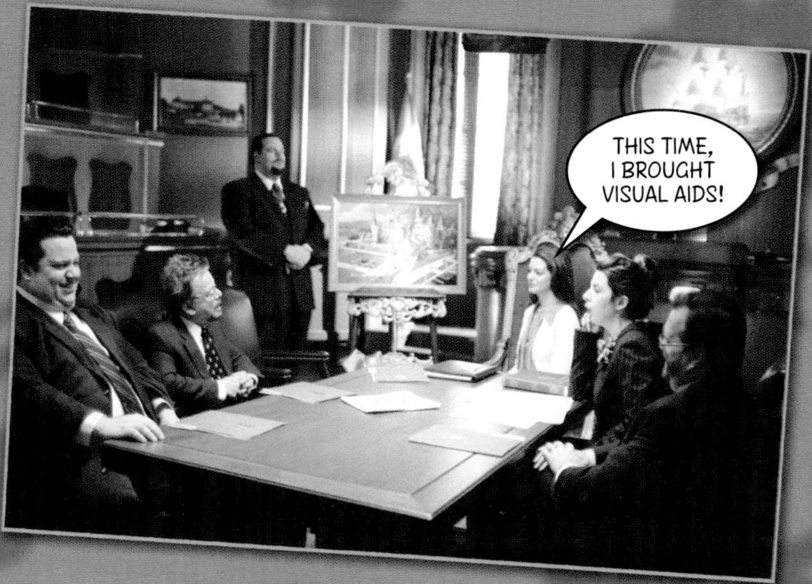
THIS TIME,
I BROUGHT
VISUAL AIDS!

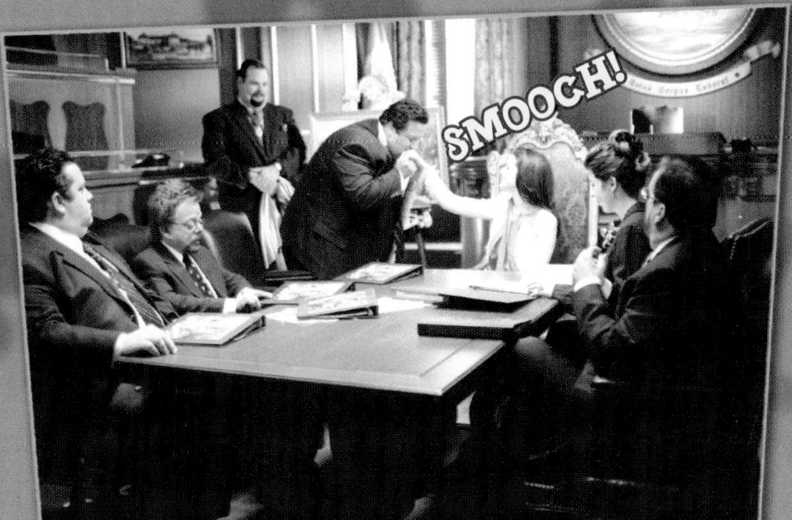
SMOOCH!

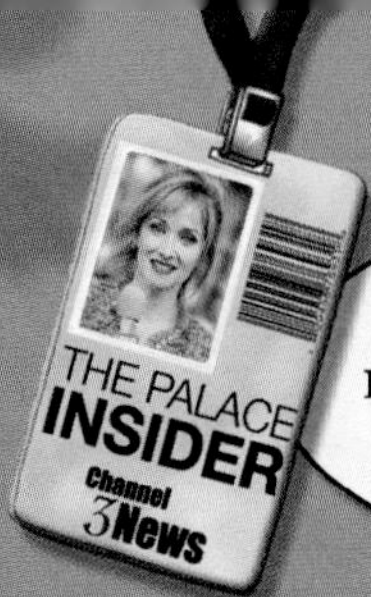
THE PALACE
INSIDER
Channel
3News

Viscount Mabrey makes an announcement in Parliament.

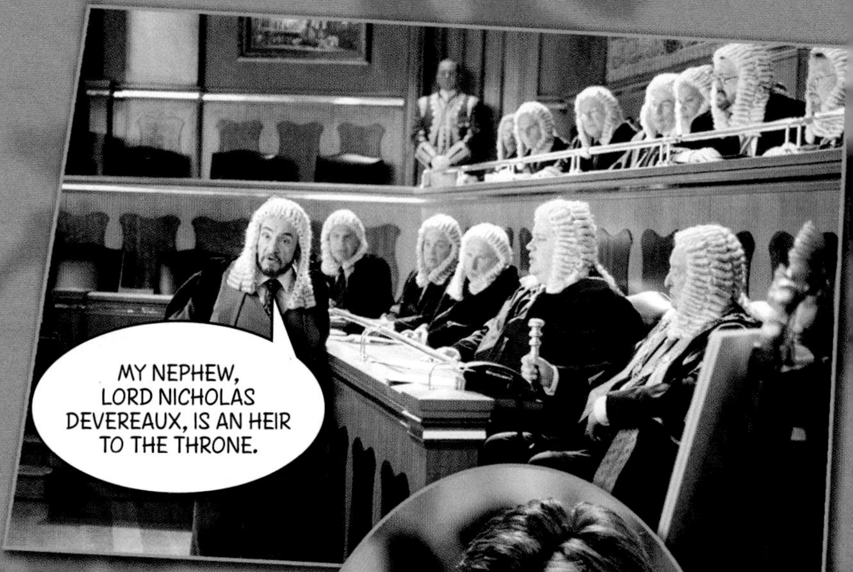
MY NEPHEW, LORD NICHOLAS DEVEREAUX, IS AN HEIR TO THE THRONE.

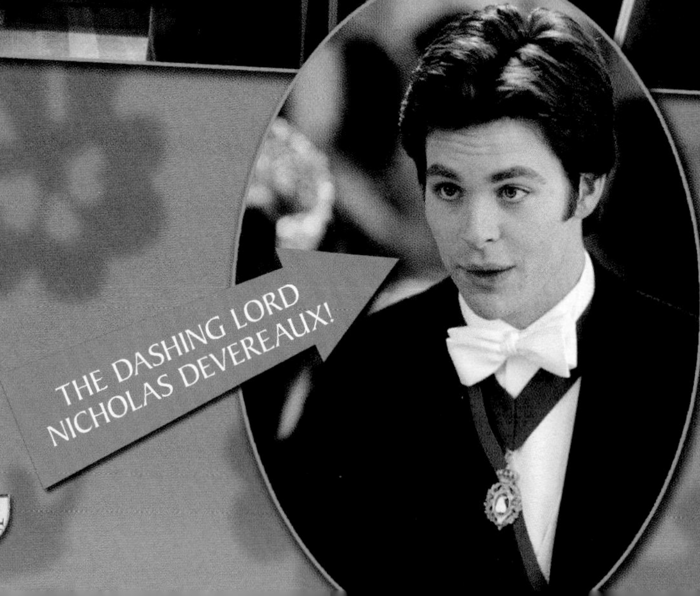
THE DASHING LORD NICHOLAS DEVEREAUX!

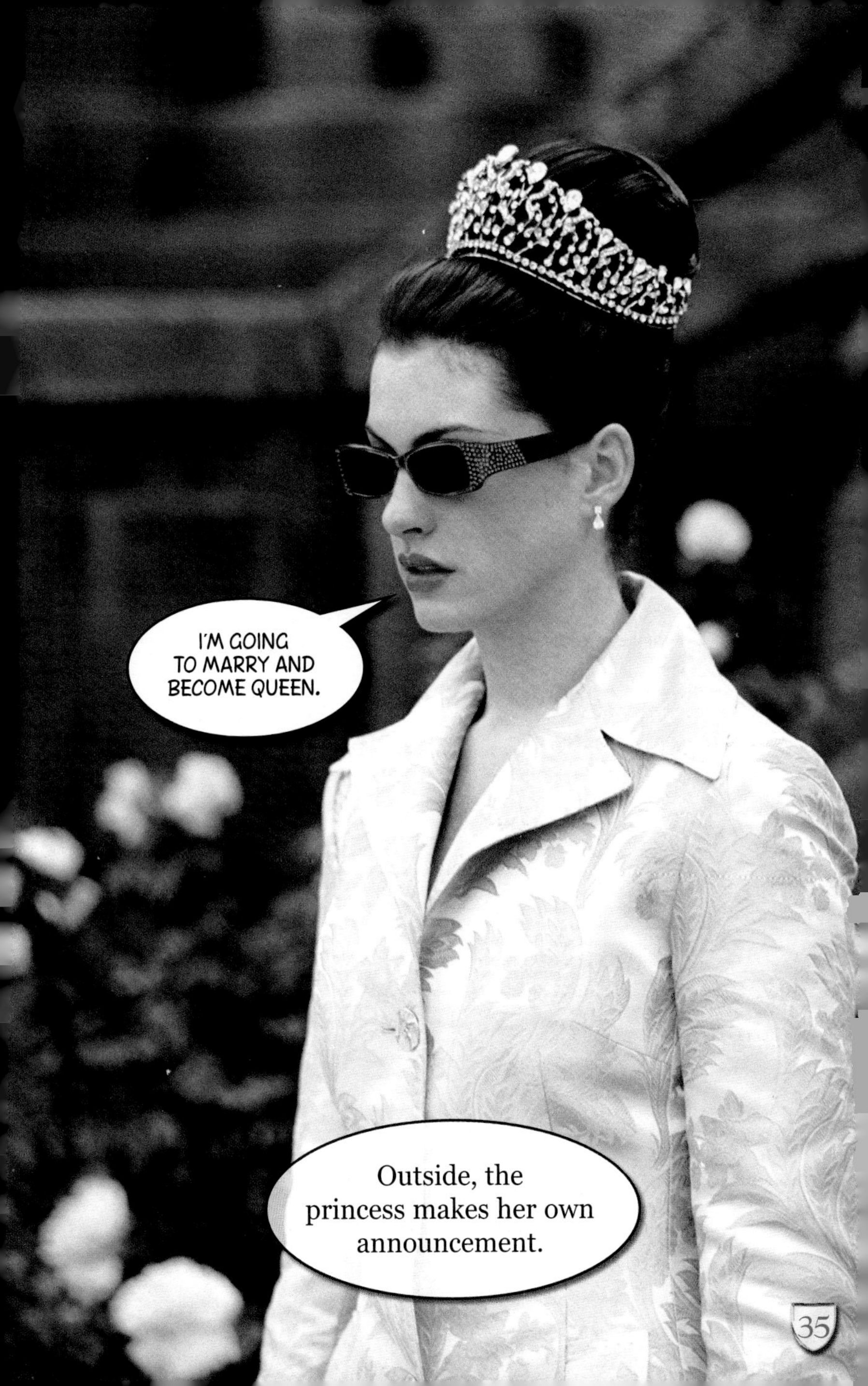
I'M GOING TO MARRY AND BECOME QUEEN.
Outside, the princess makes her own announcement.

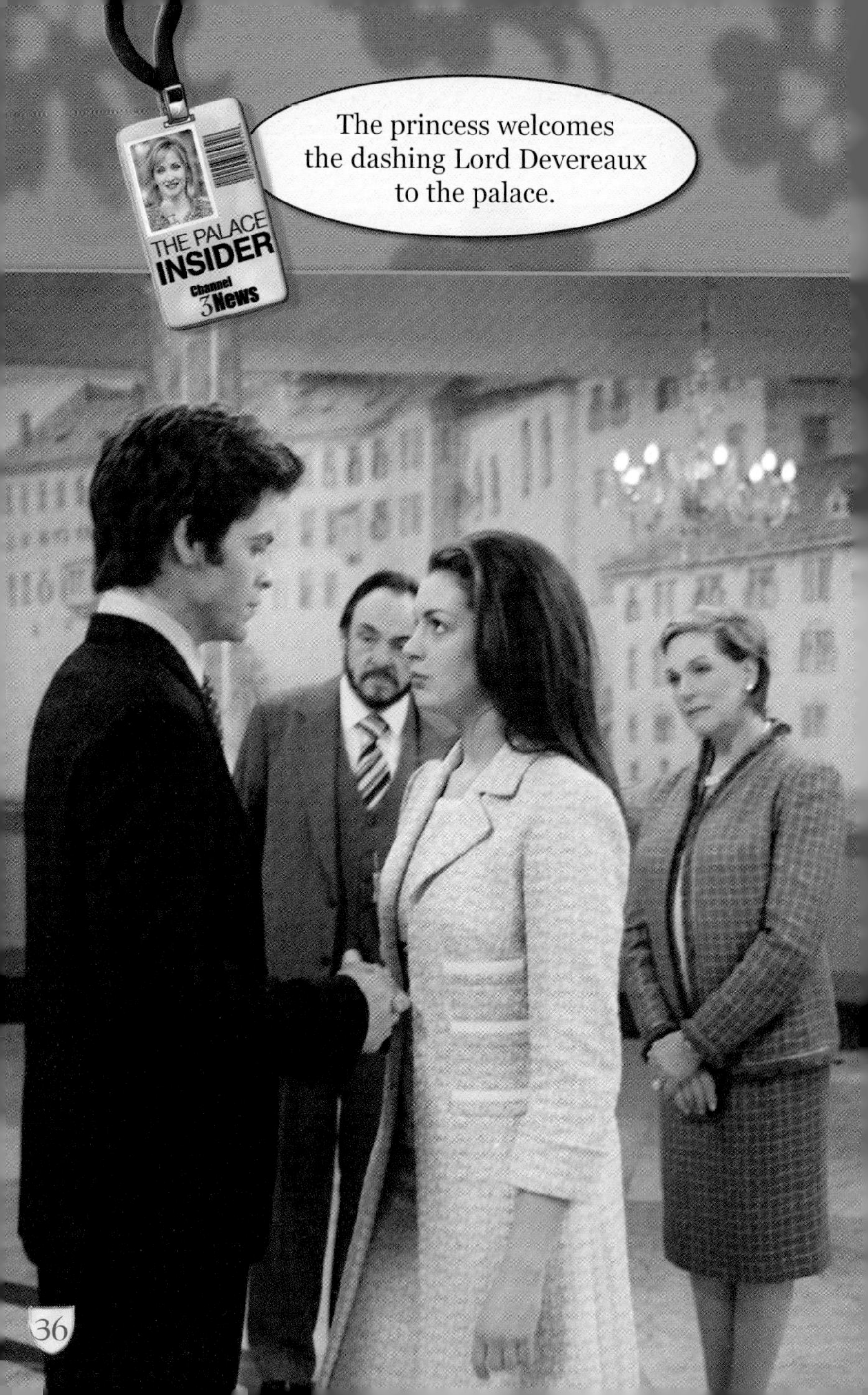
The princess welcomes the dashing Lord Devereaux to the palace.
THE PALACE INSIDER
Channel 3News

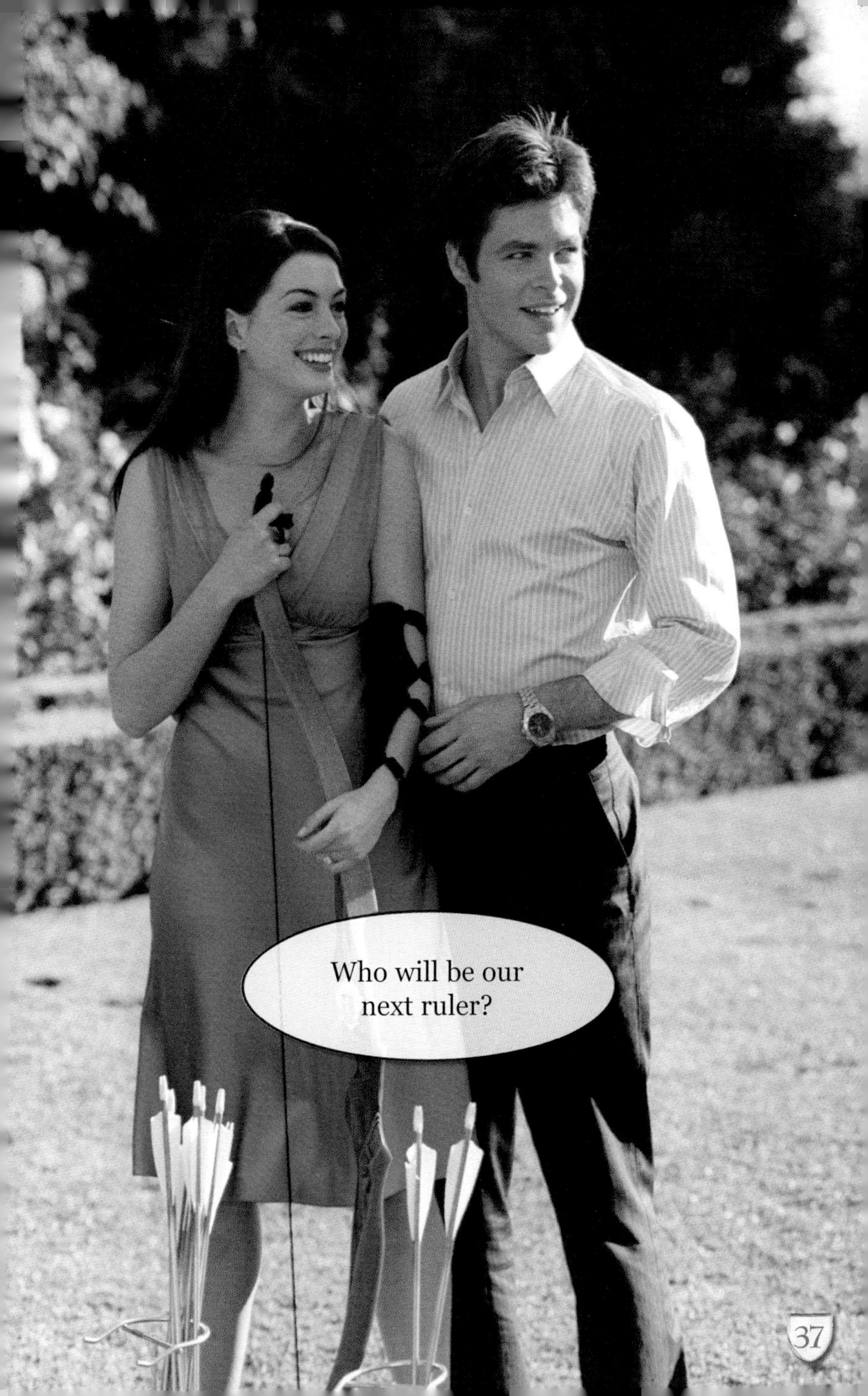
Who will be our next ruler?

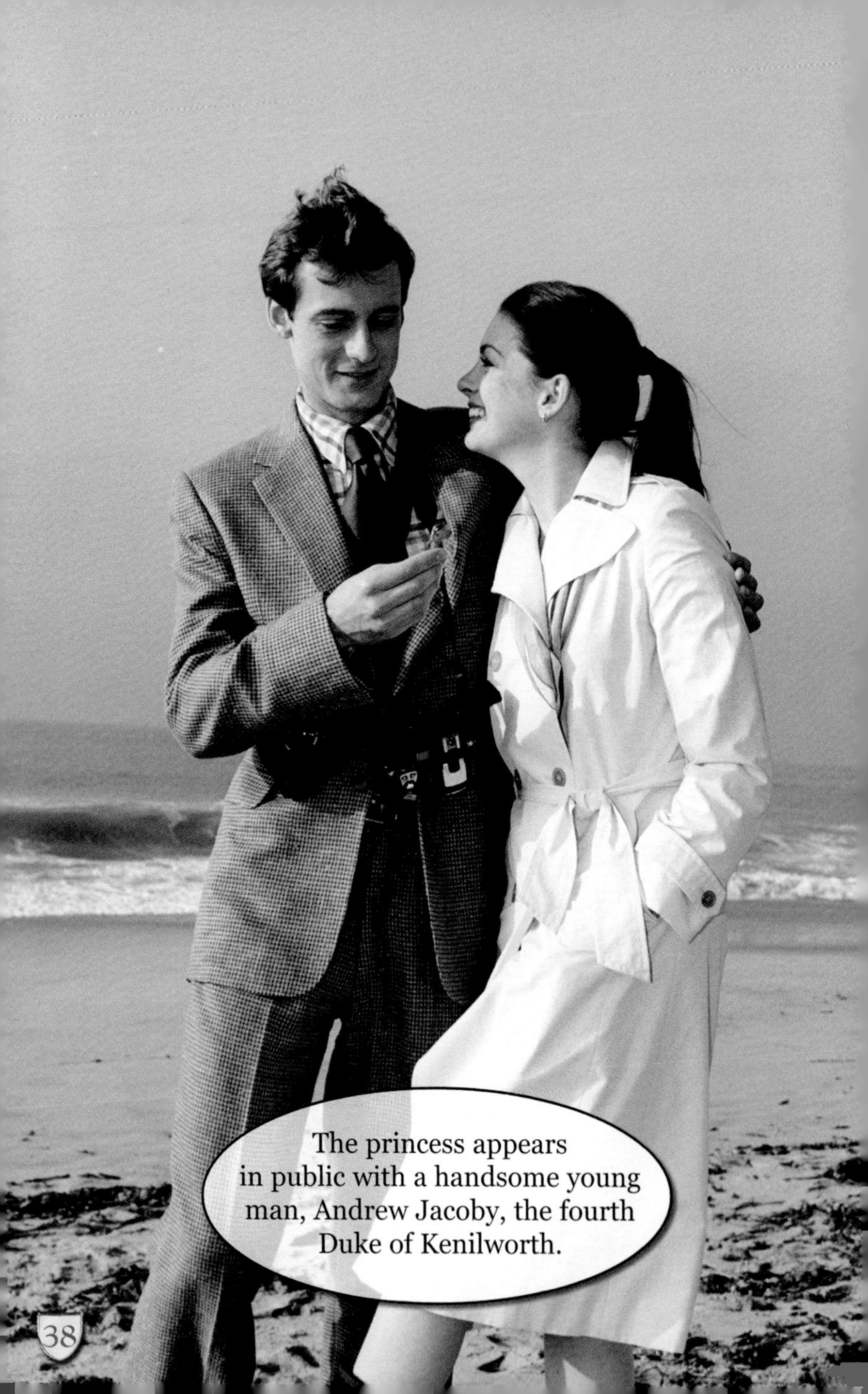

The princess appears in public with a handsome young man, Andrew Jacoby, the fourth Duke of Kenilworth.

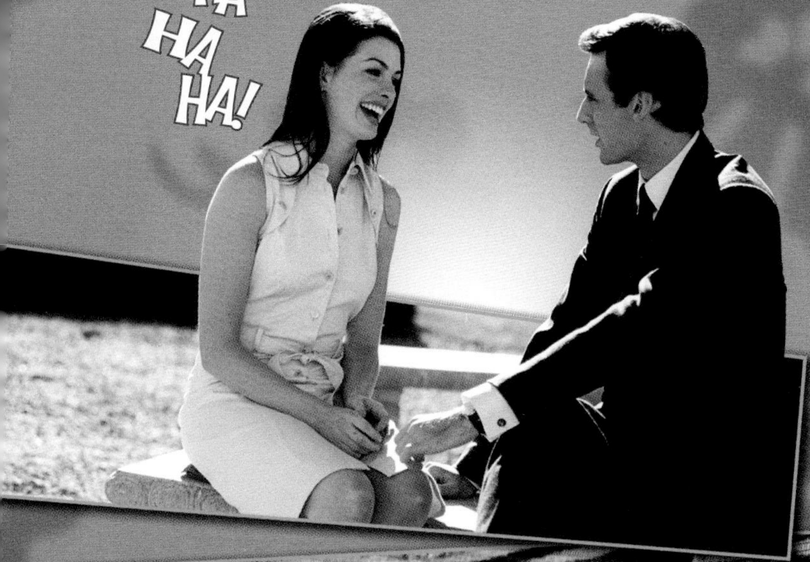
HA
HA
HA!
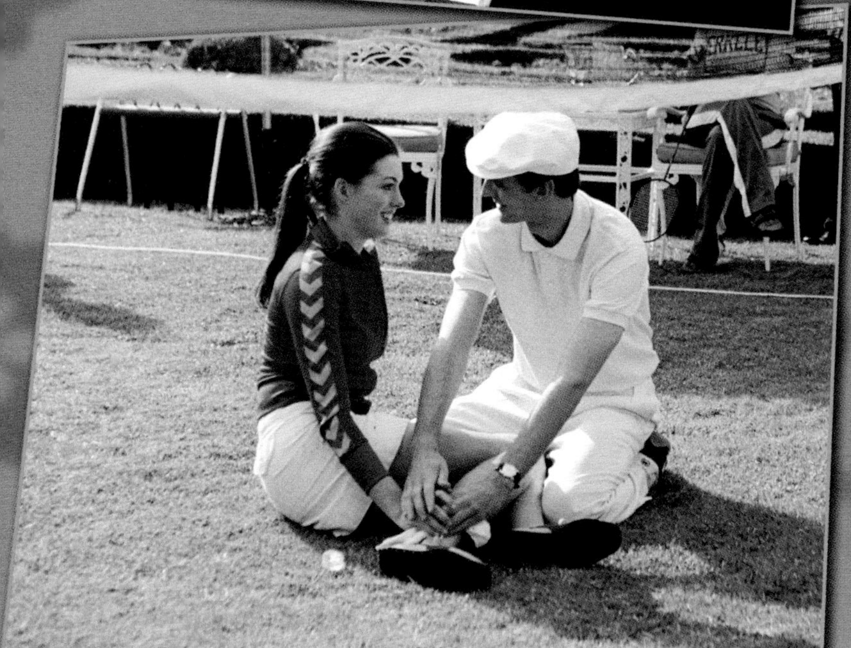

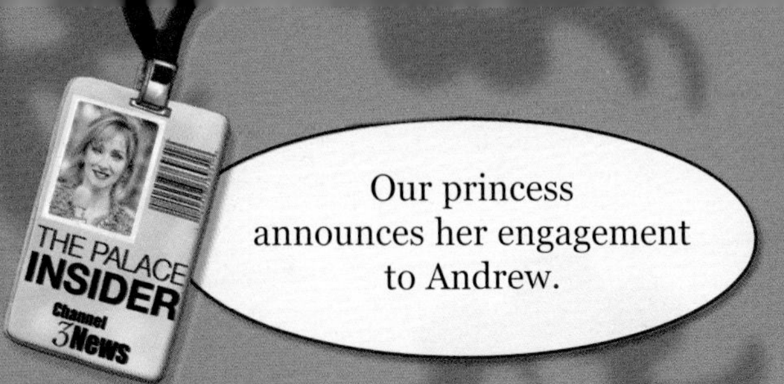
THE PALACE
INSIDER
Channel
3News
Our princess announces her engagement to Andrew.

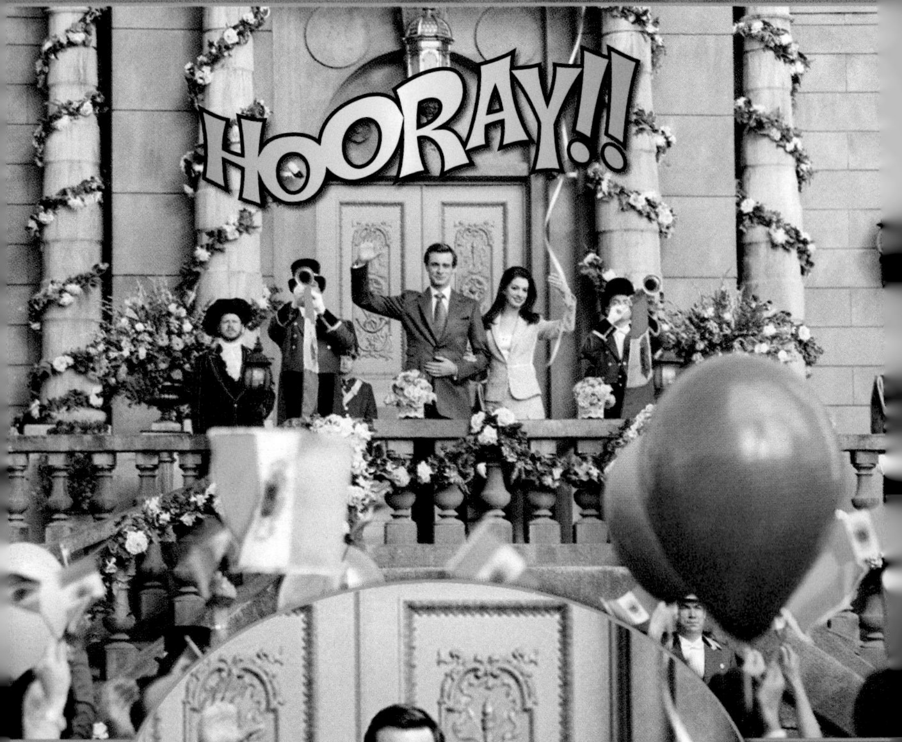
HOORAY!!

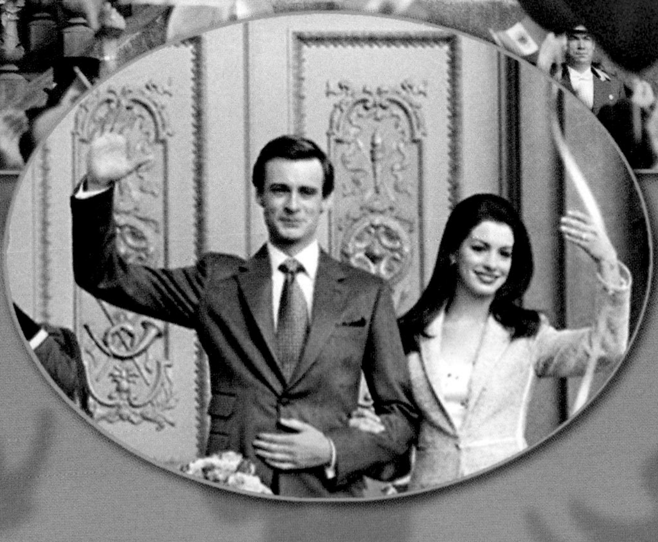

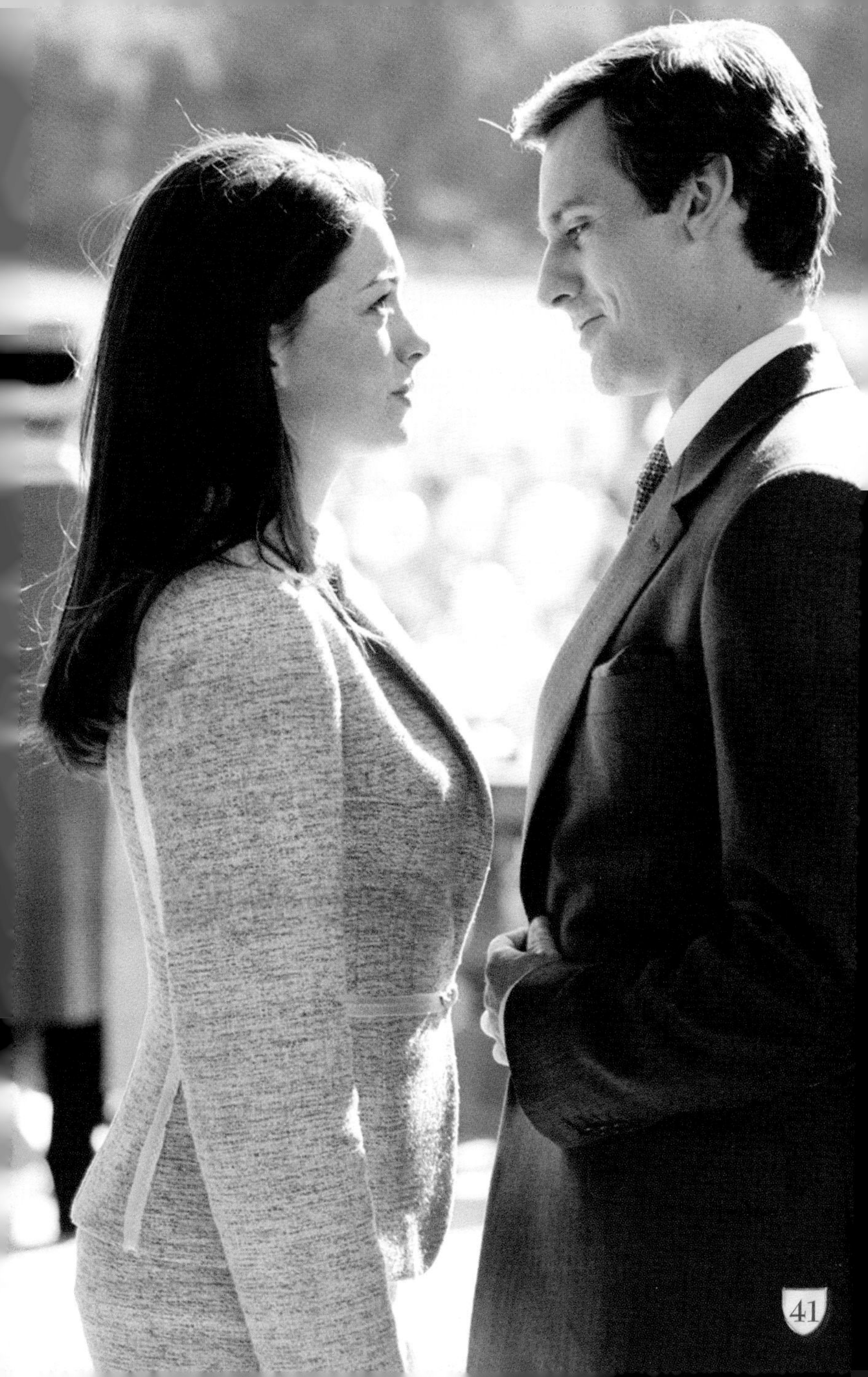

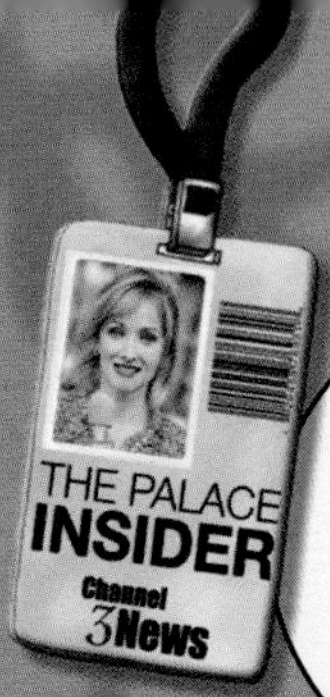
THE PALACE
INSIDER
Channel
3News

The Palace Insider attends the Queen's Royal Tea in the palace gardens. The princess makes the rounds with her best friend Lilly Moscovitz and, of course, her handsome fiancé. Lord Nicholas Devereaux arrives with Elissa Wells.

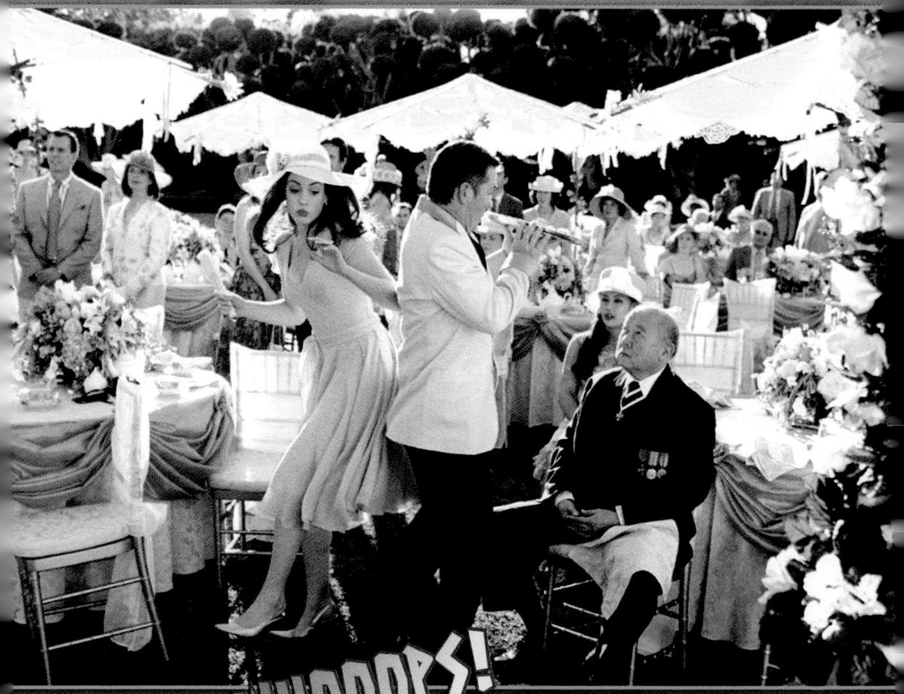

WHOOOPS!

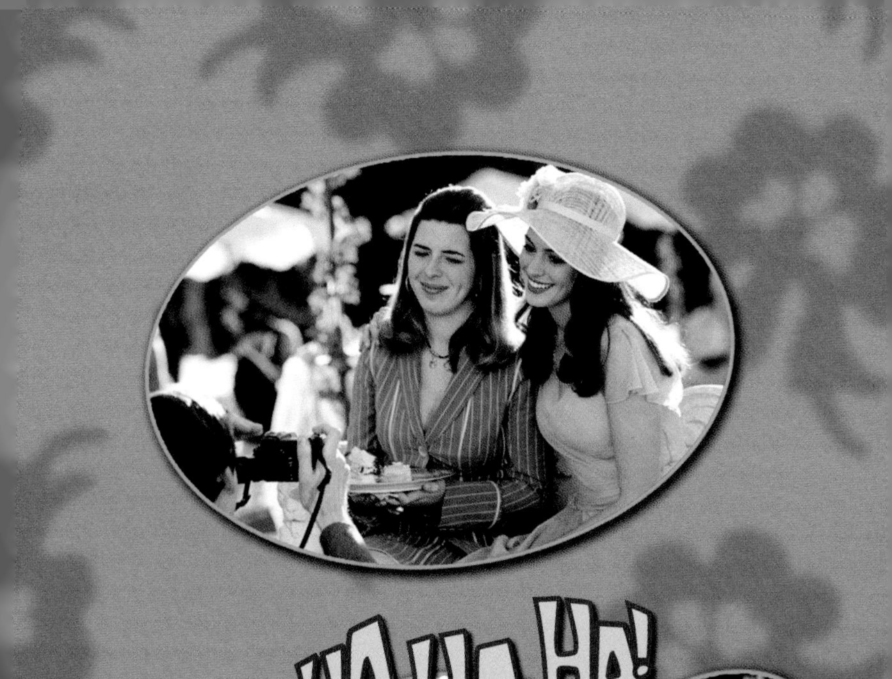

HA HA HA!

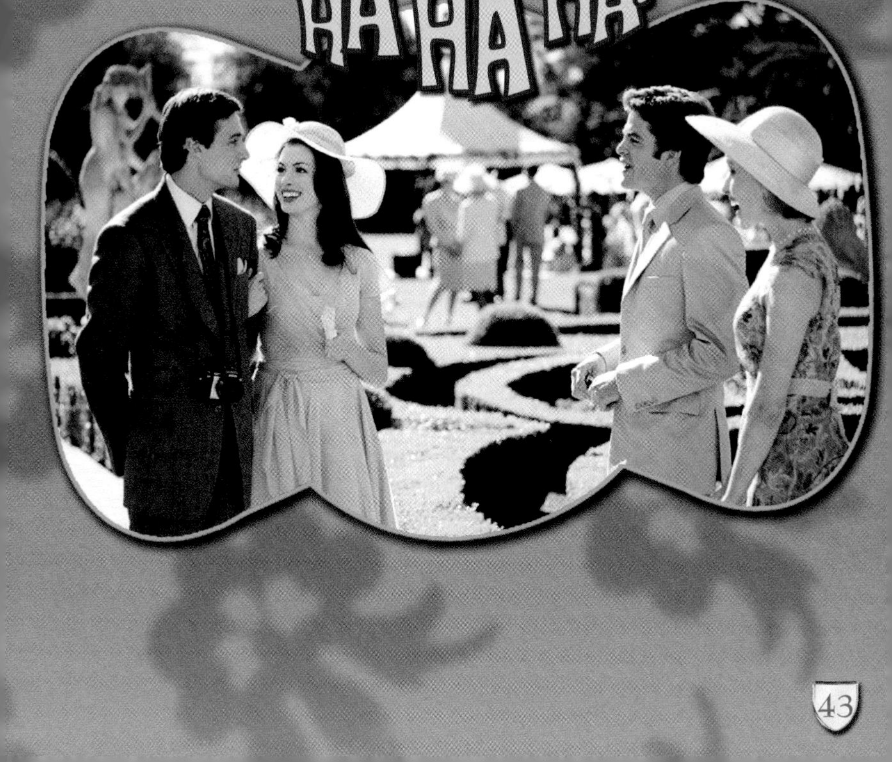

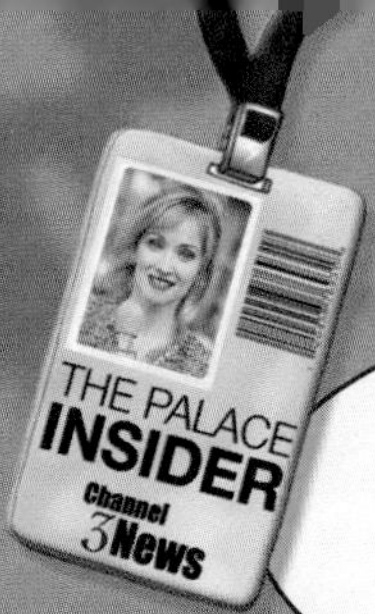
THE PALACE
INSIDER
Channel
3News

The dashing Lord Nicholas Devereaux finds time to speak with our princess. The Palace Insider snaps these exclusive photos!

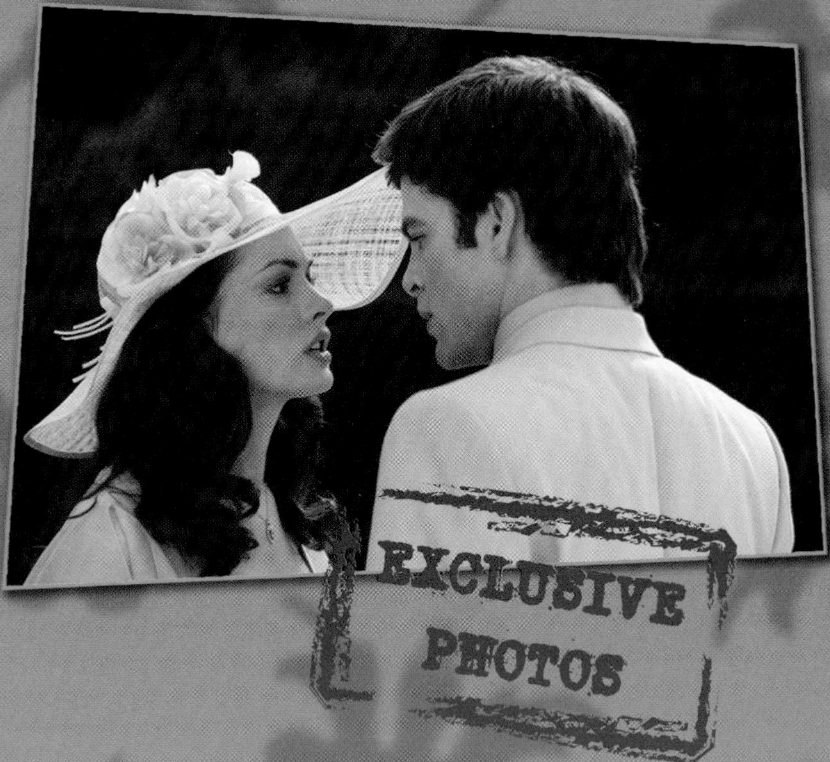
EXCLUSIVE
PHOTOS

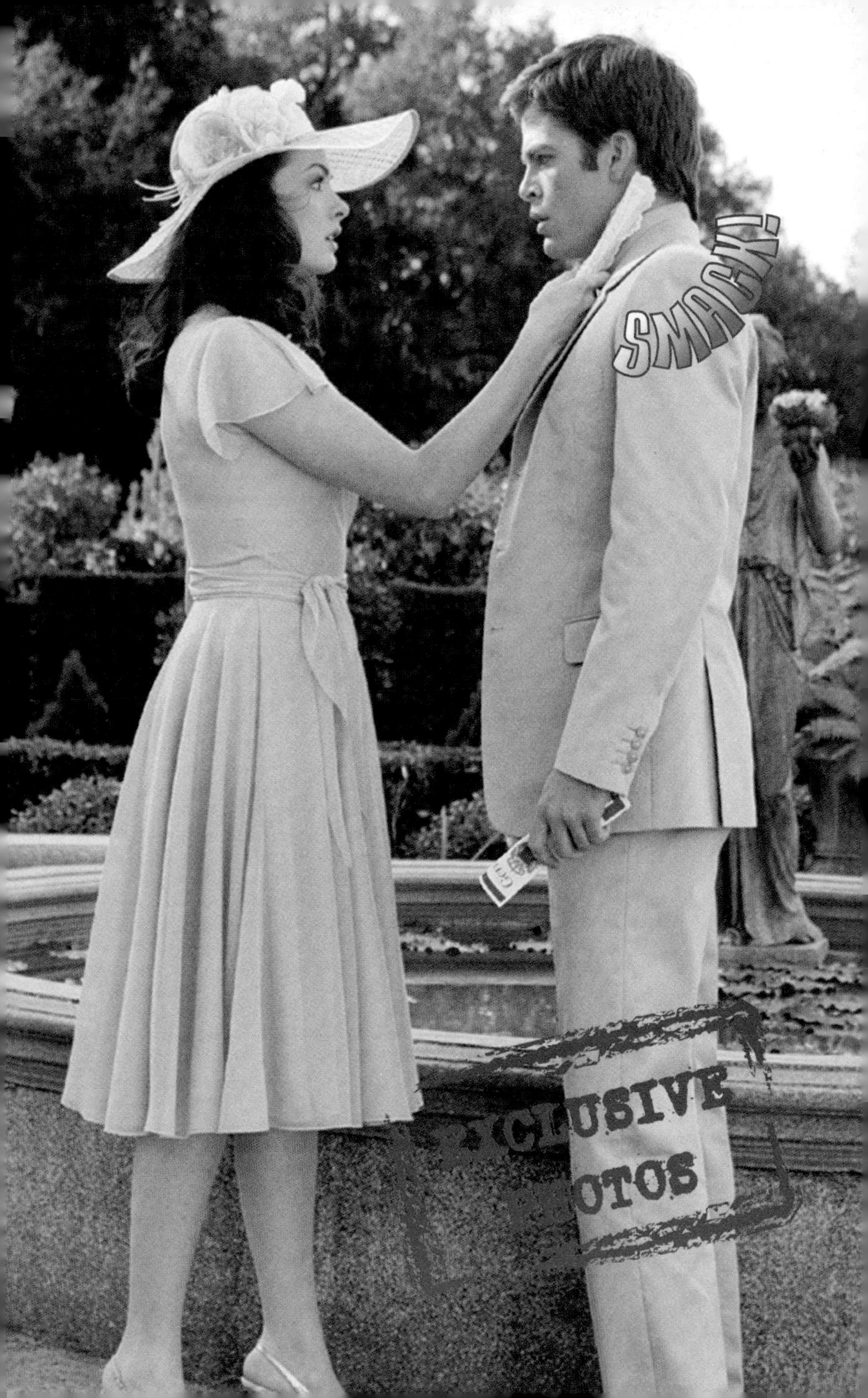
SMACK!
CLUSIVE
OTOS

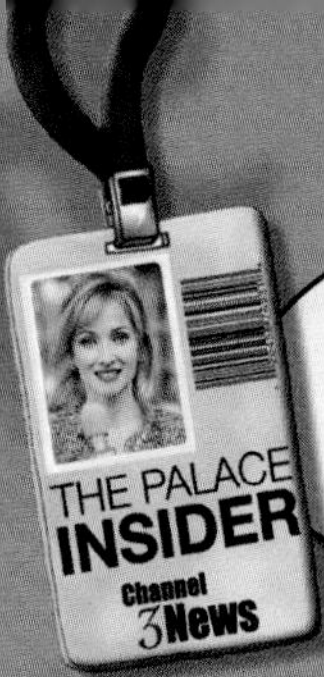
THE PALACE
INSIDER
Channel
3News

Princesses from all over the globe enjoy a royal bridal shower at the Genovian palace. One of the foreign princesses plays Palace Insider to get these photos!

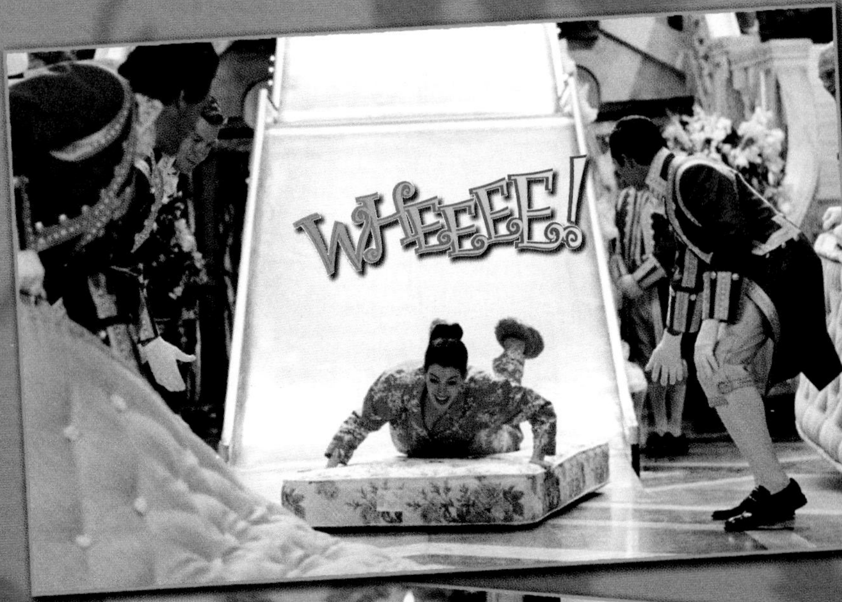
WHEEEE!

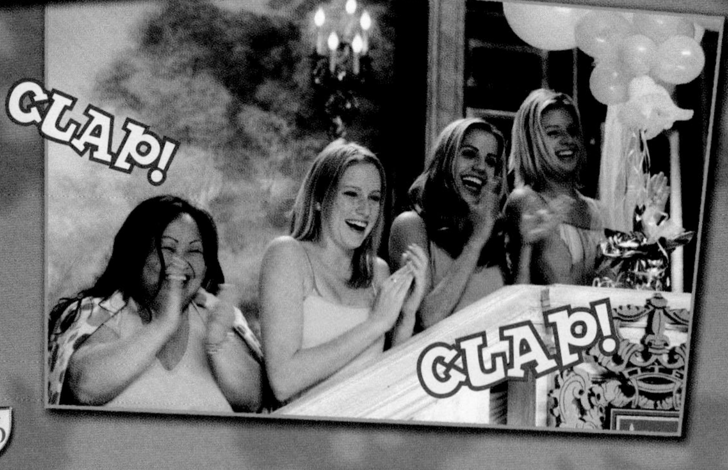
CLAP!
CLAP!

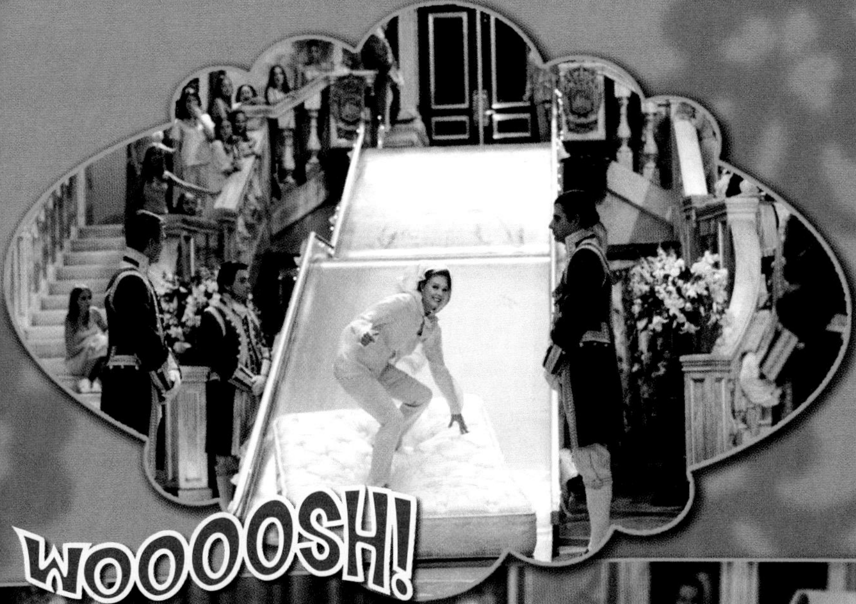
WOOOOSH!

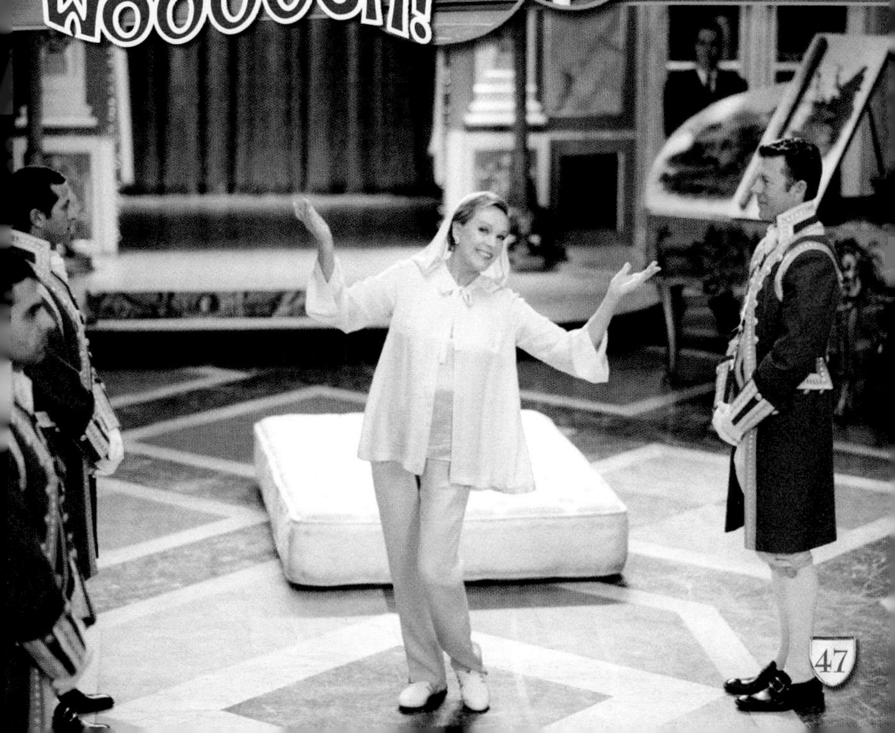

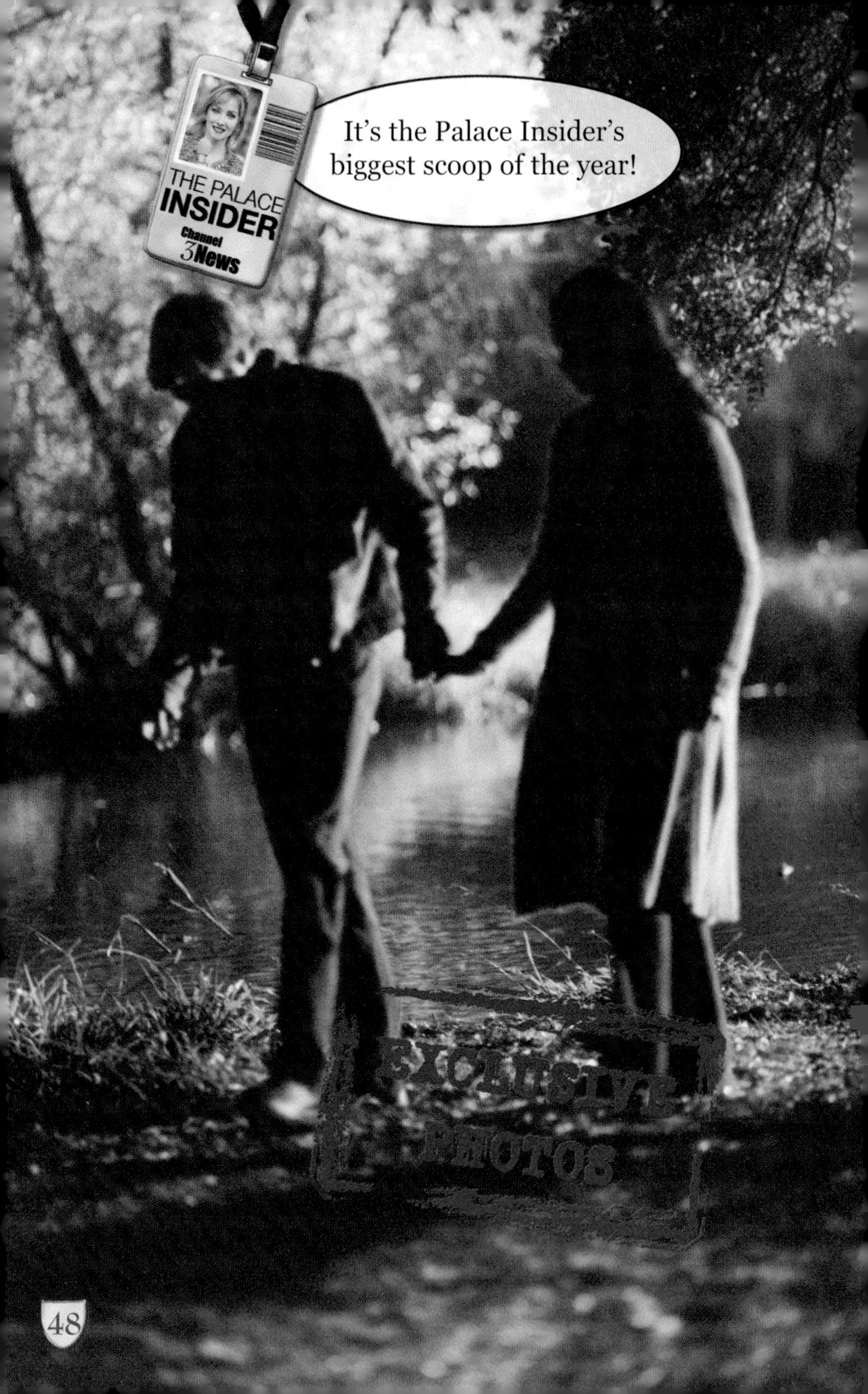
THE PALACE INSIDER
Channel 3News
It's the Palace Insider's biggest scoop of the year!

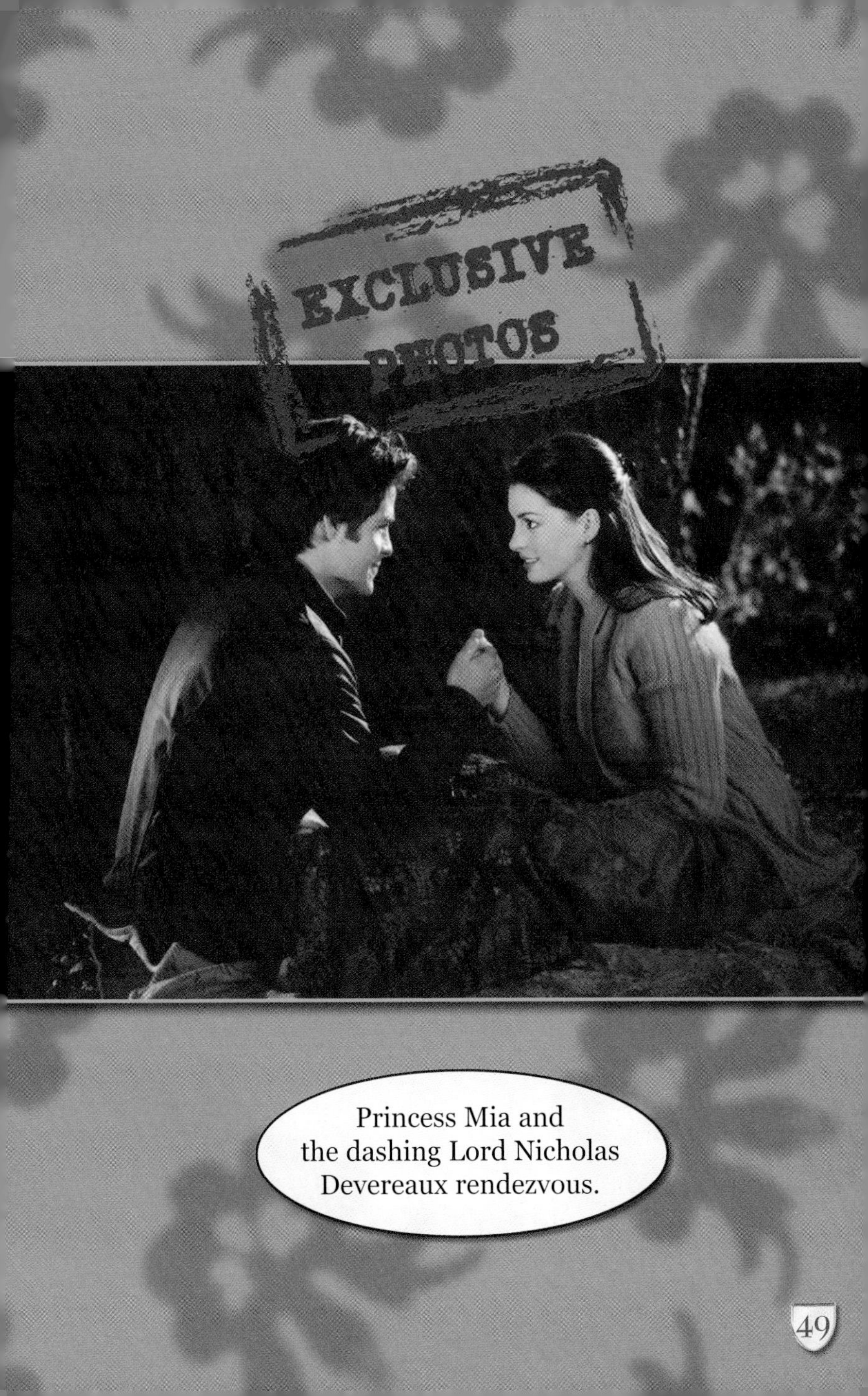
EXCLUSIVE
PHOTOS

Princess Mia and
the dashing Lord Nicholas
Devereaux rendezvous.

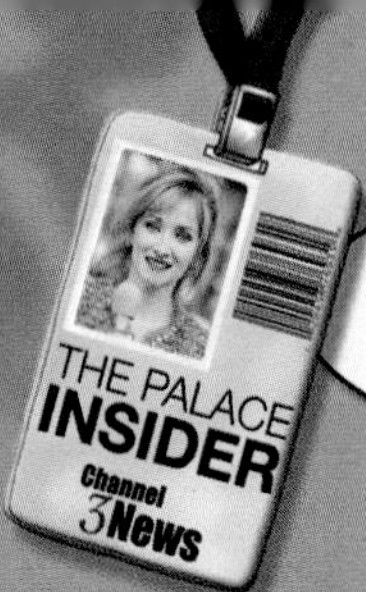
THE PALACE
INSIDER
Channel
3News

The princess rides off in a hurry.

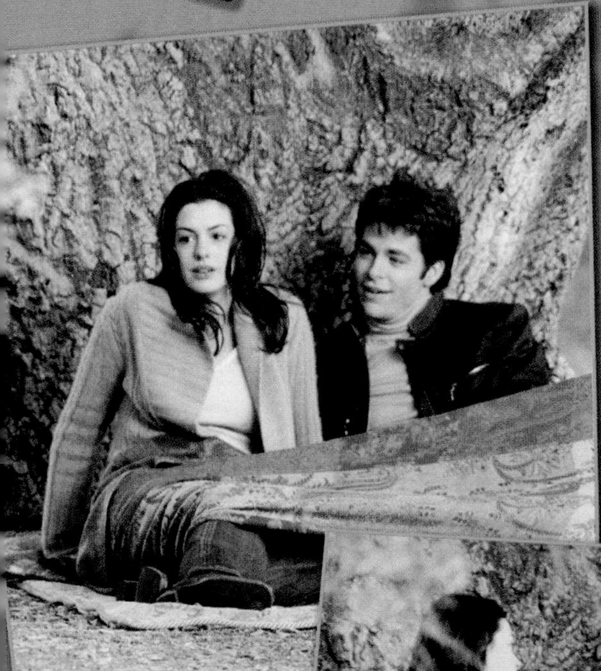

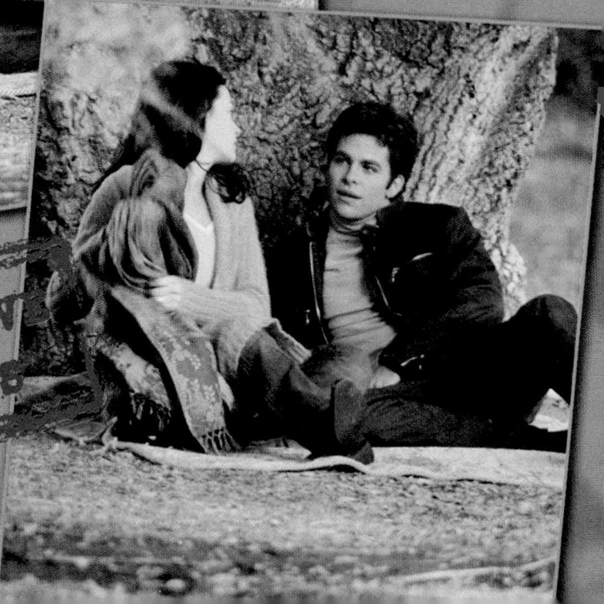

EXCLUSIVE PHOTOS

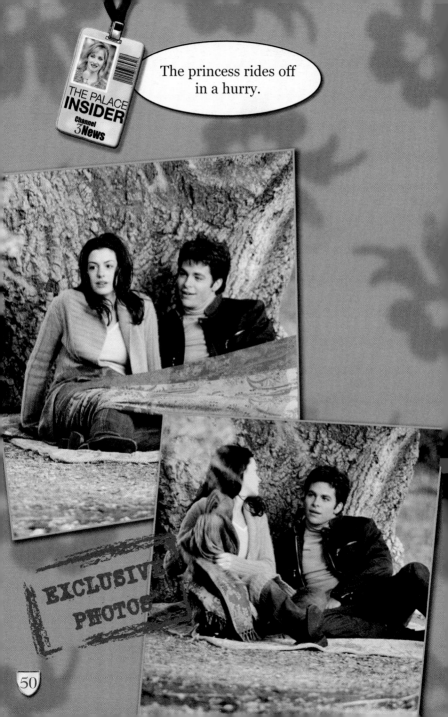

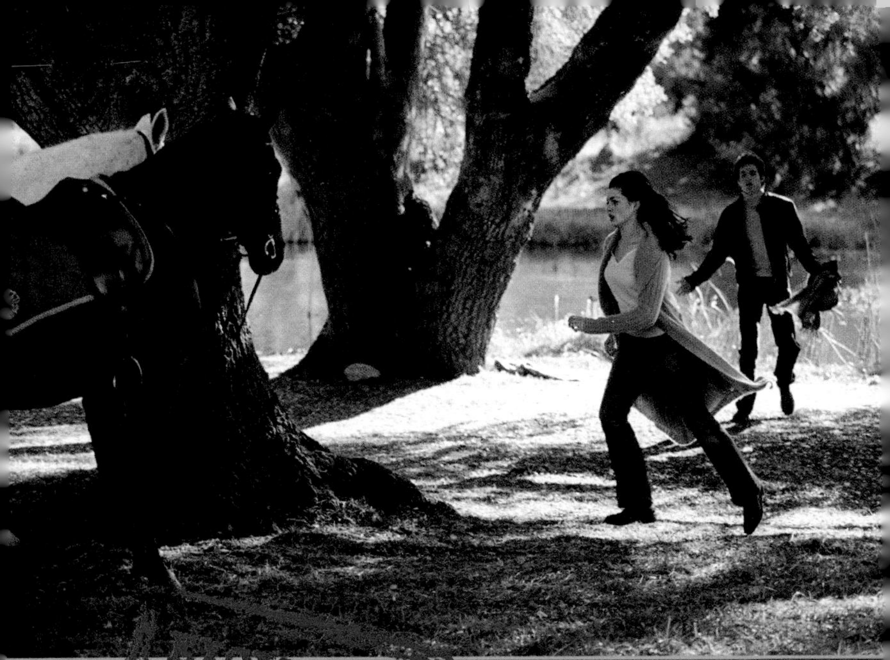

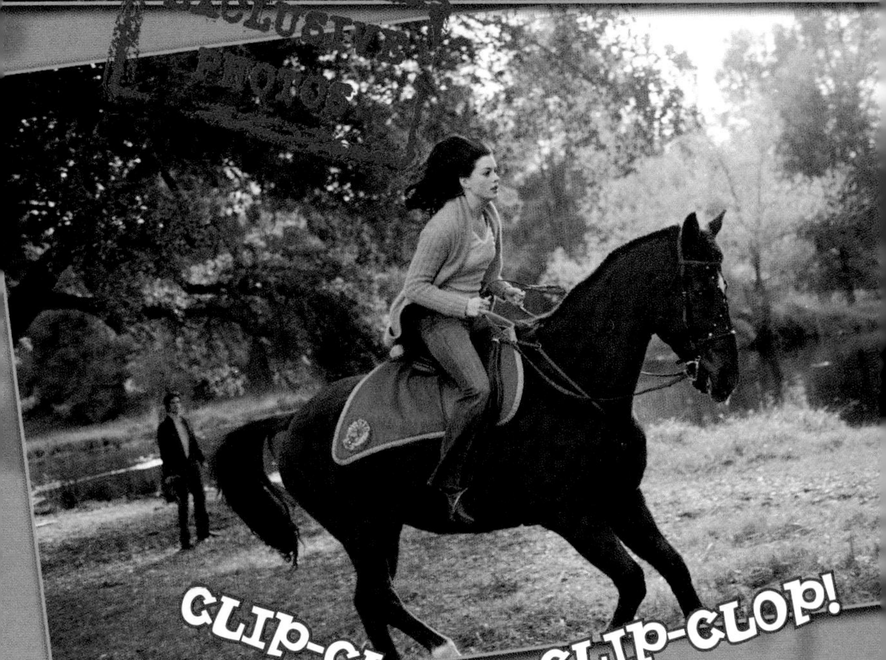
EXCLUSIVE PHOTOS
CLIP-CLOP!
CLIP-CLOP!

THE PALACE
INSIDER
Channel
3News

The wedding's on!
In Genovia's National Cathedral,
maid of honor Lilly Moscovitz
moves down the aisle in her
strange American way.

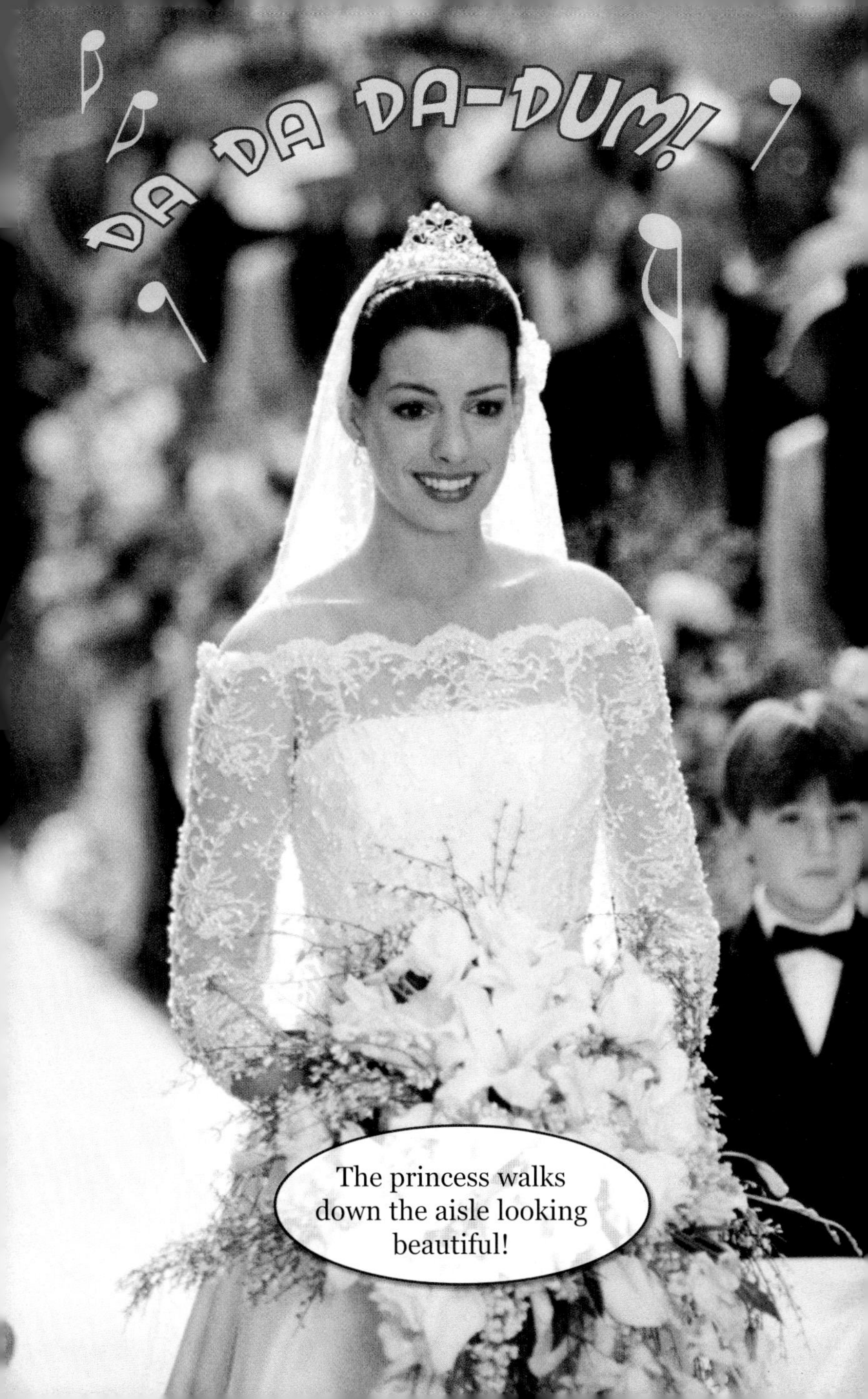
DA DA DA-DUM!
The princess walks down the aisle looking beautiful!

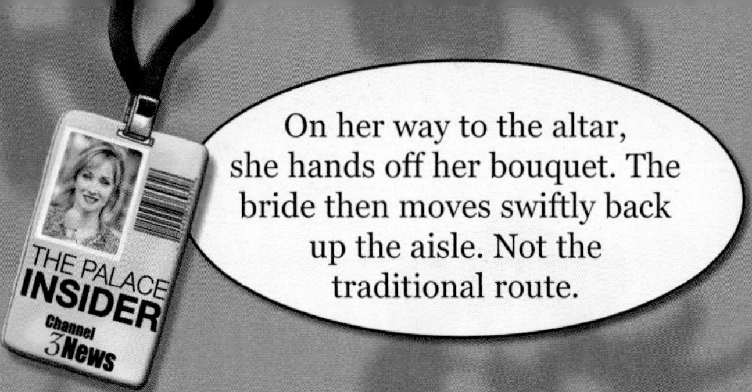
On her way to the altar, she hands off her bouquet. The bride then moves swiftly back up the aisle. Not the traditional route.
THE PALACE INSIDER
Channel 3News

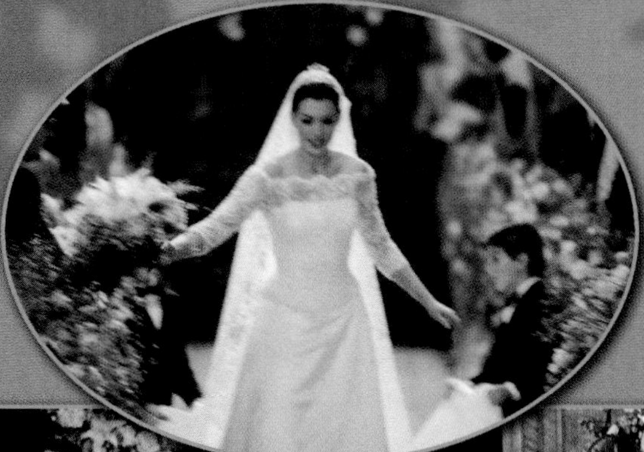

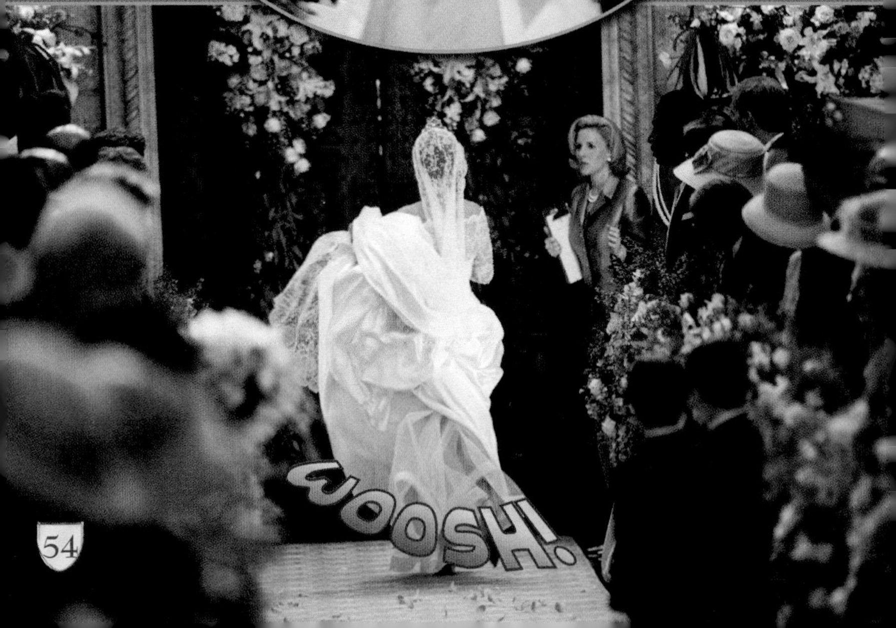
WOOSH!

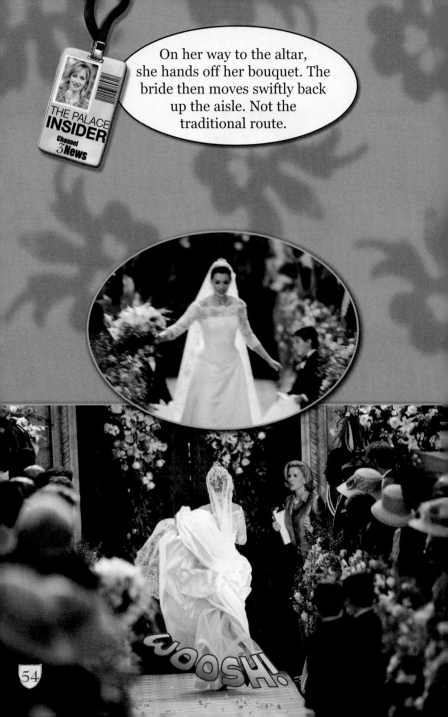

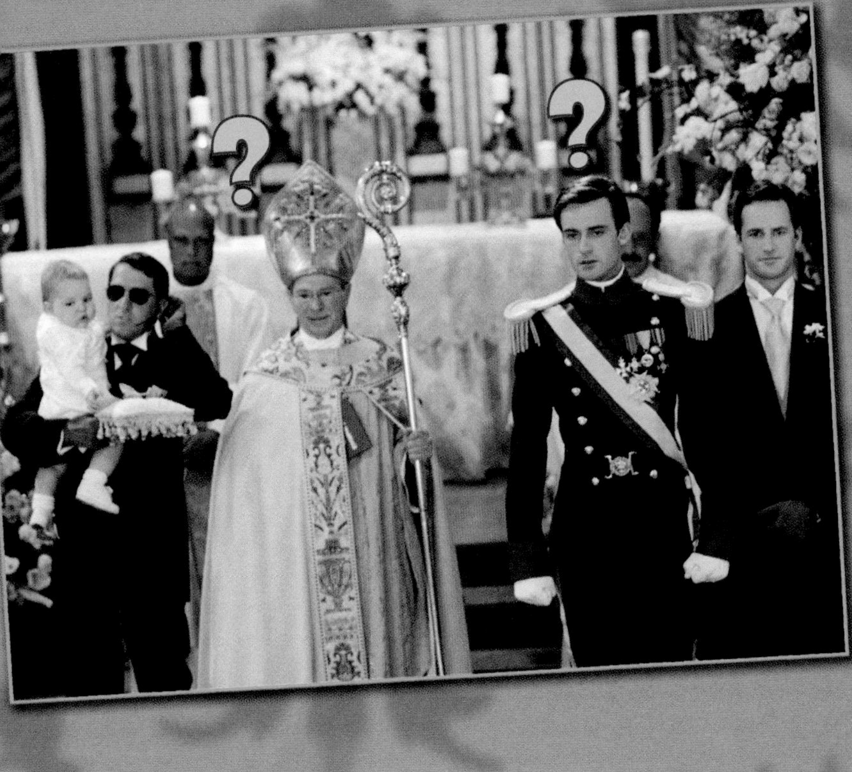
?
?

Where's the bride?

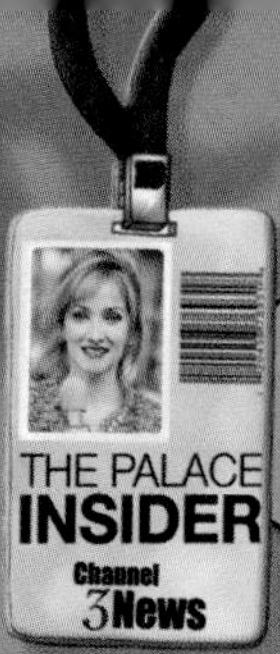
THE PALACE
INSIDER
Channel
3News

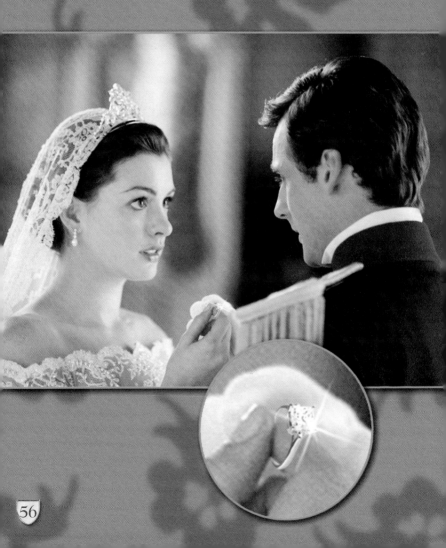

The bride's back in the church, and...uh-oh! She gives her ring—that big diamond ring!—back to the groom! Oh goodness!

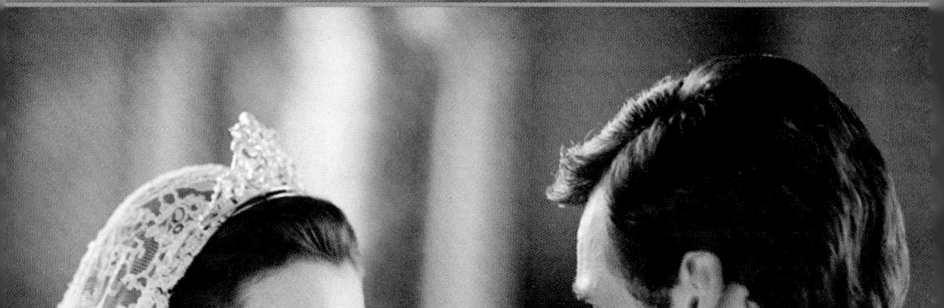

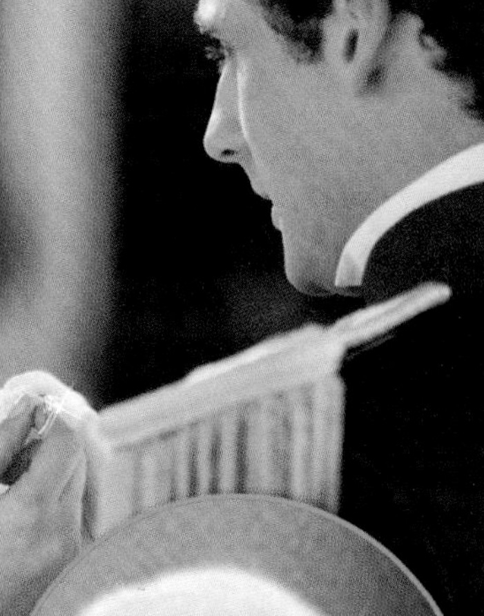

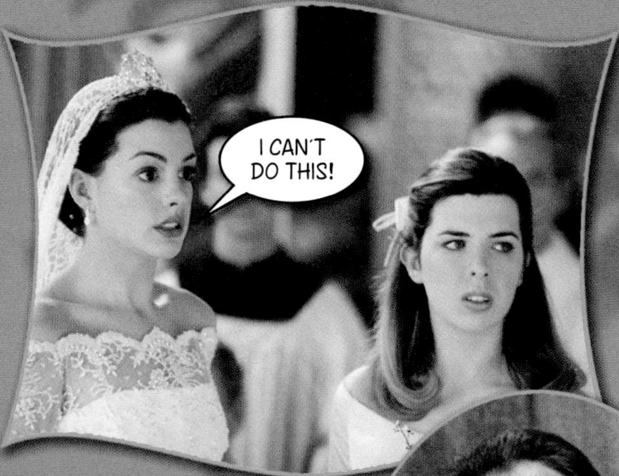
I CAN'T DO THIS!

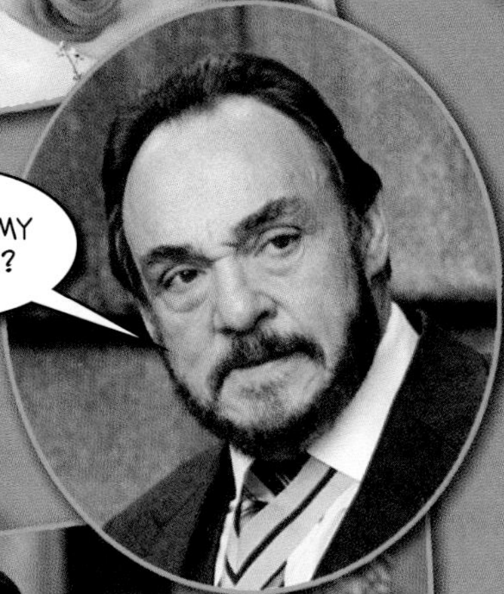
WHERE'S MY NEPHEW?

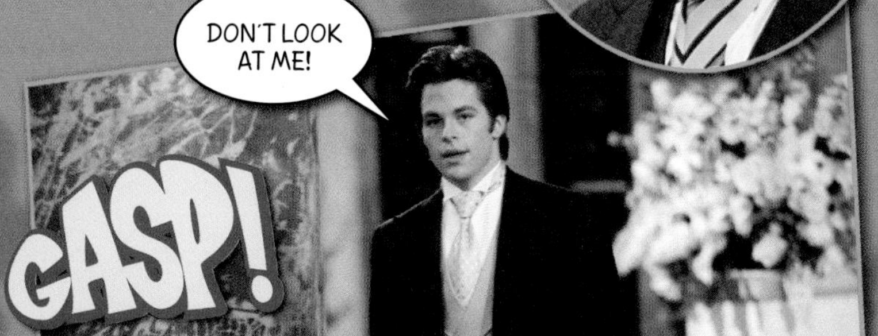
DON'T LOOK AT ME!
GASP!

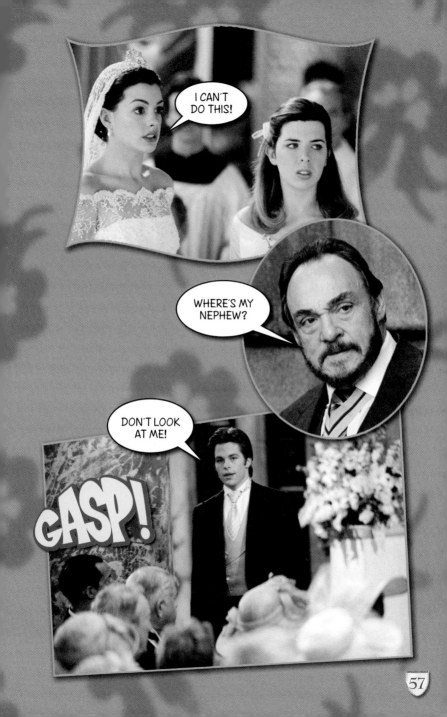

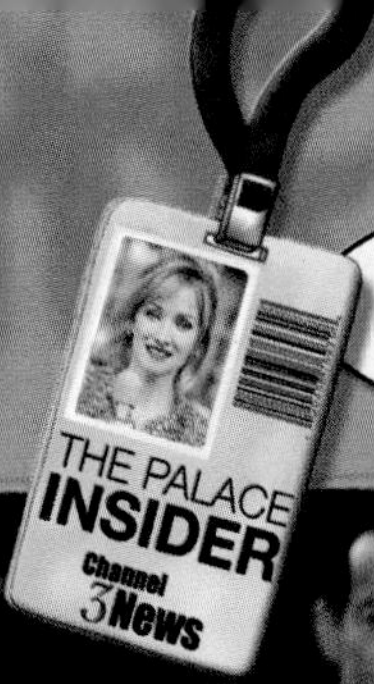
THE PALACE INSIDER
Channel 3 News
Parliament votes to repeal the marriage law!

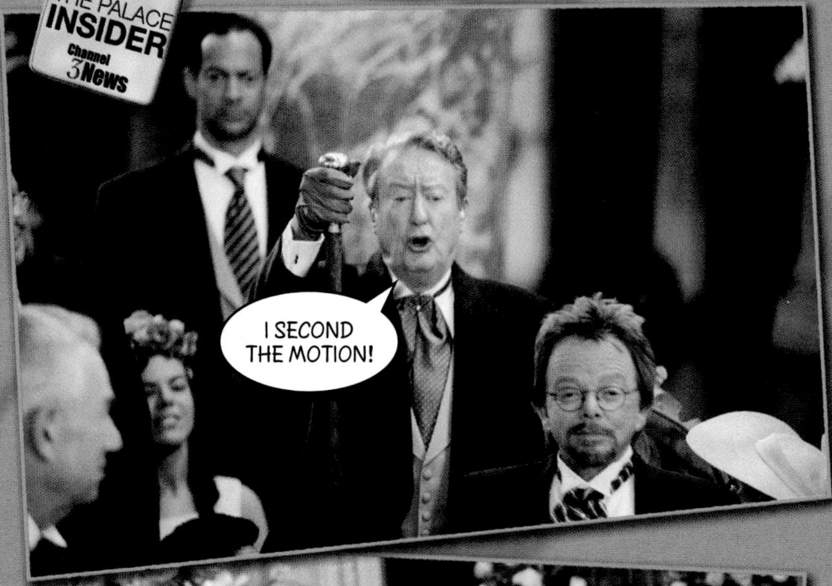
I SECOND THE MOTION!

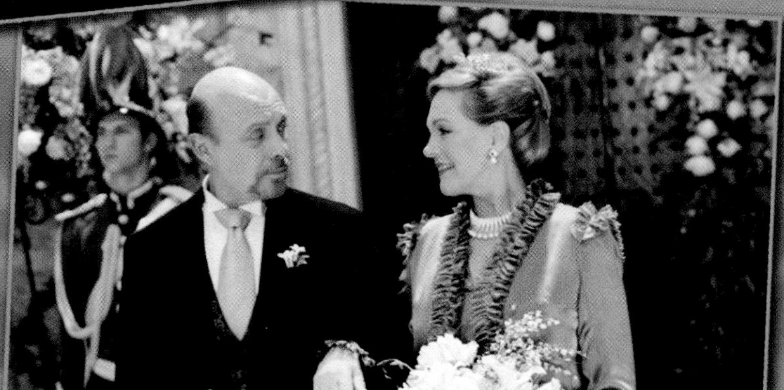

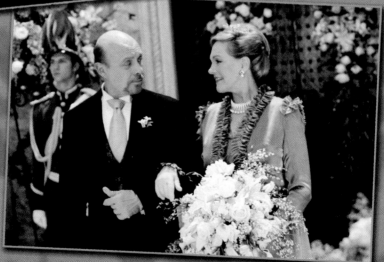

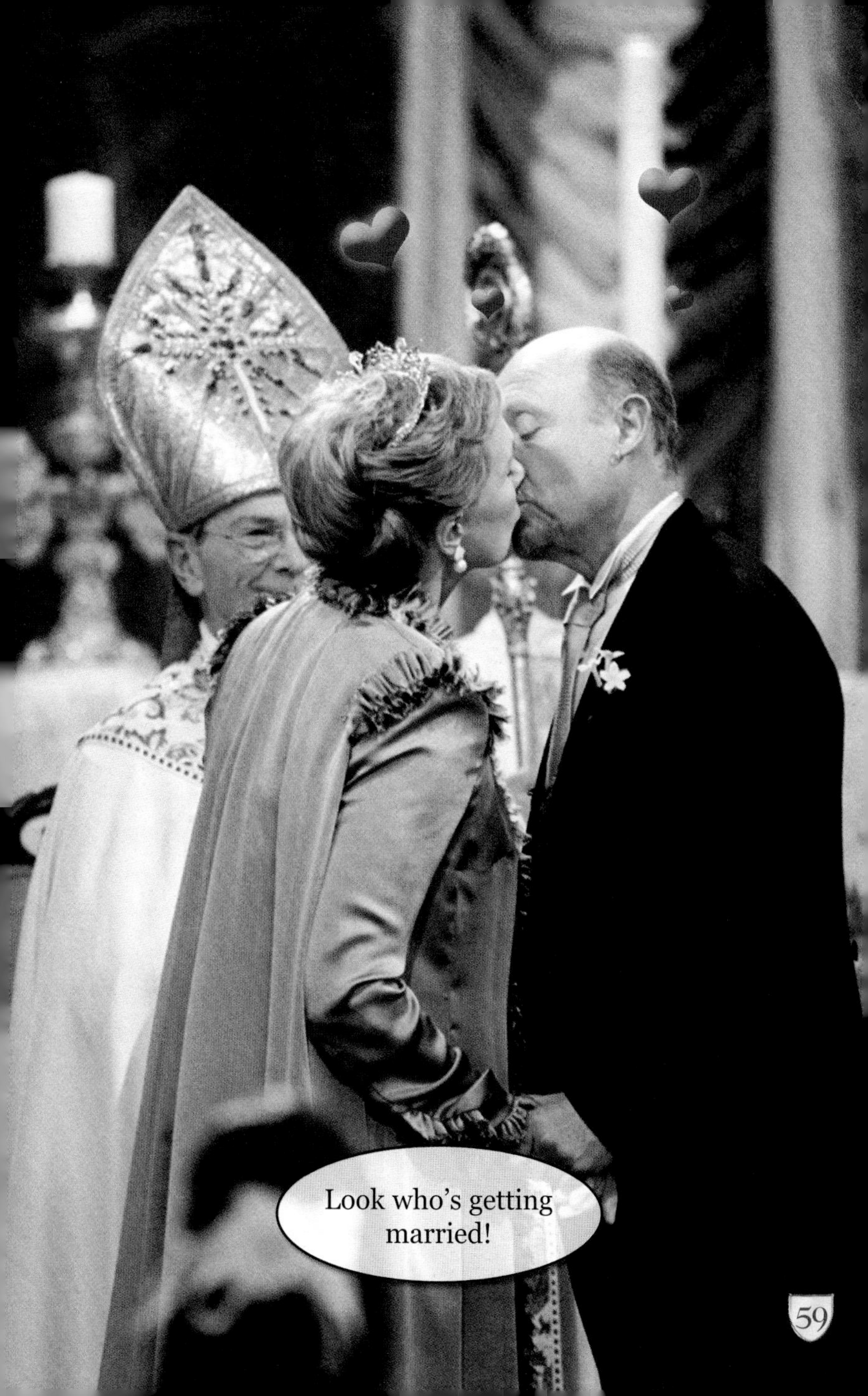
Look who's getting married!

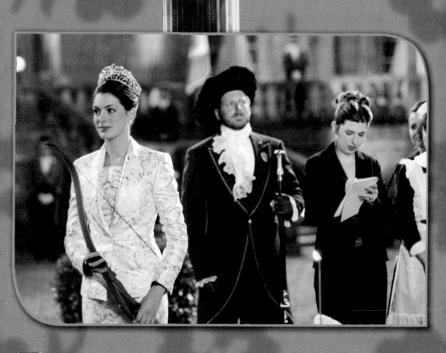

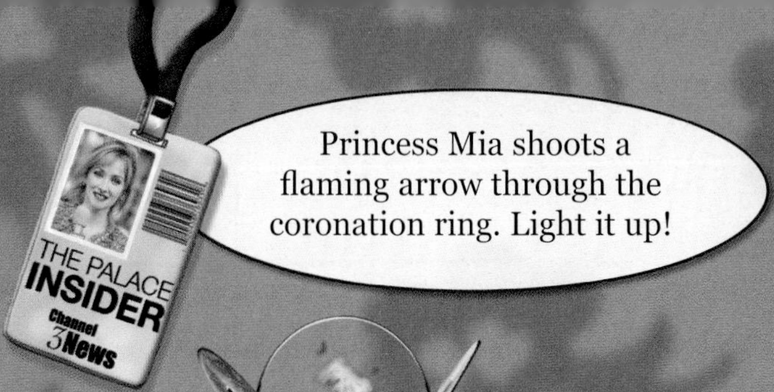
Princess Mia shoots a flaming arrow through the coronation ring. Light it up!
THE PALACE INSIDER
Channel 3 News

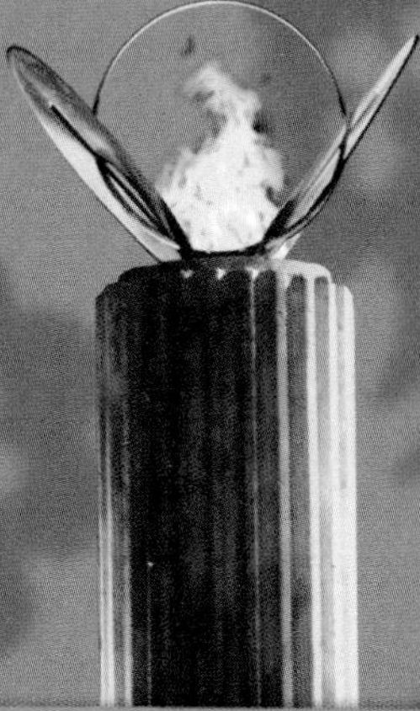

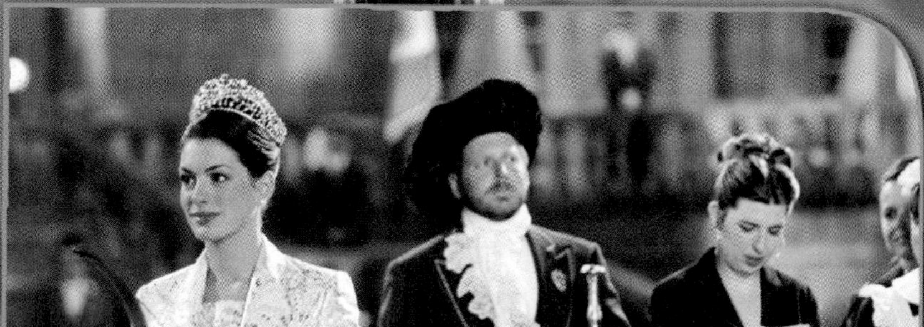

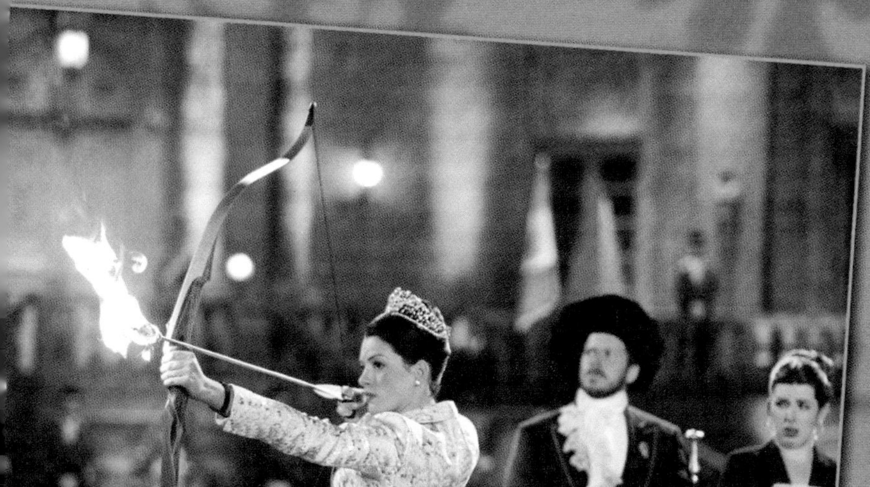
TWANG!

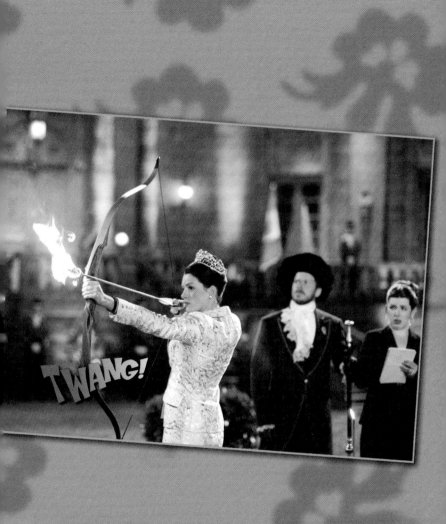

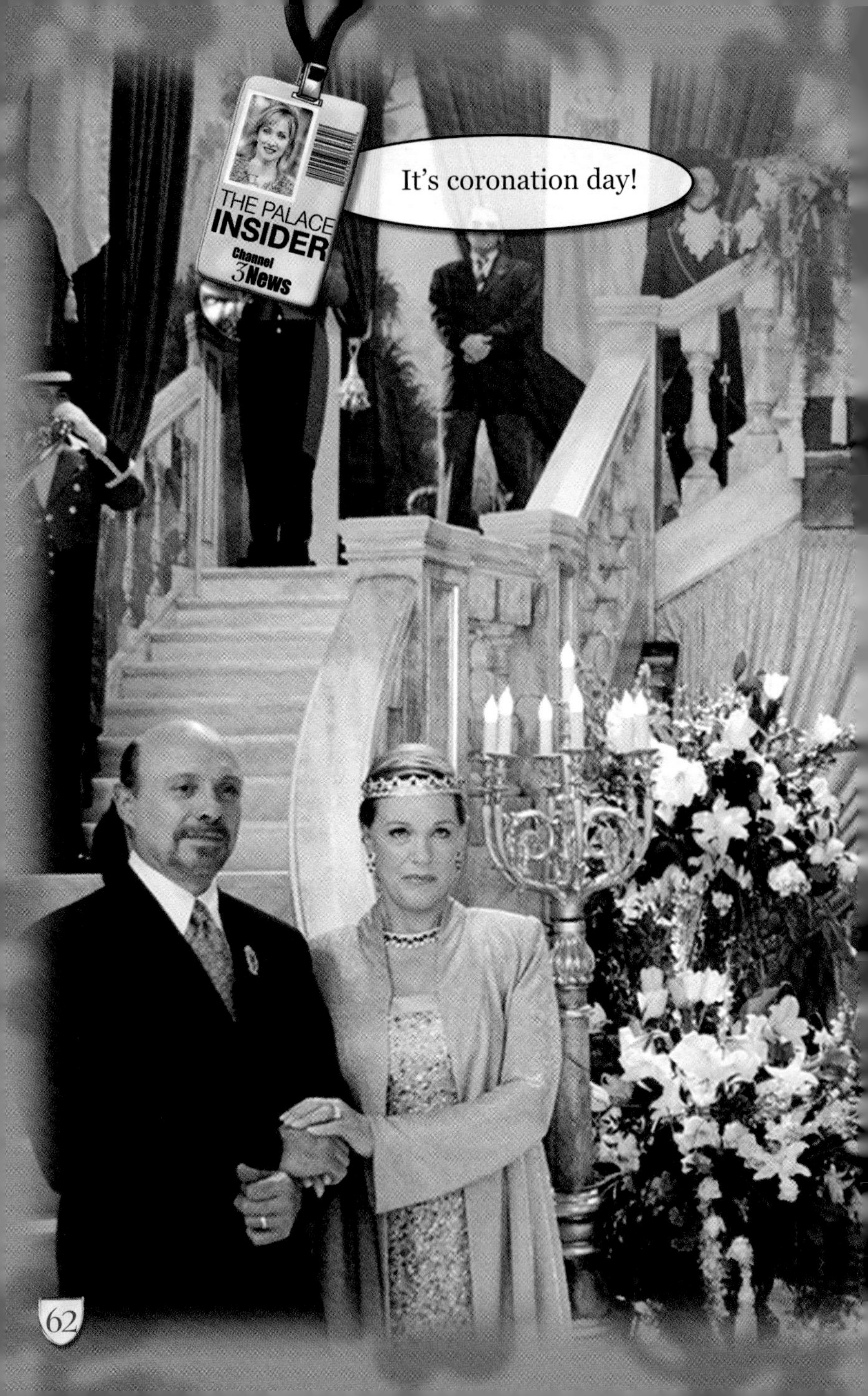
THE PALACE
INSIDER
Channel
3News
It's coronation day!

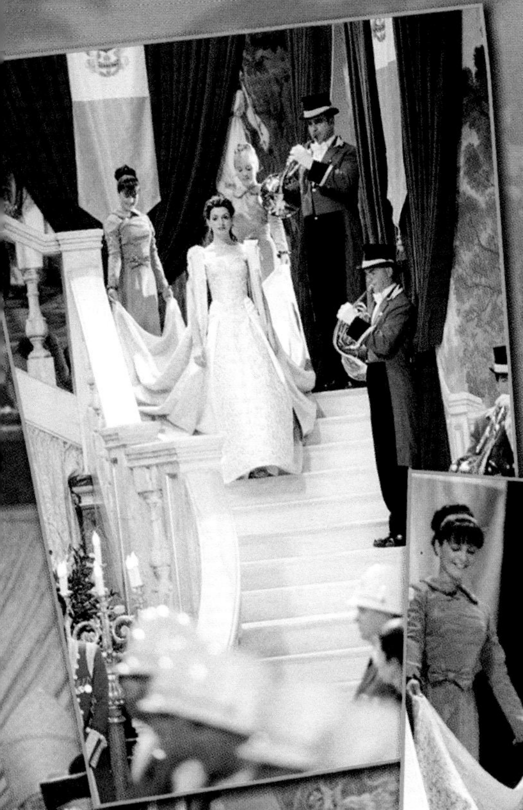

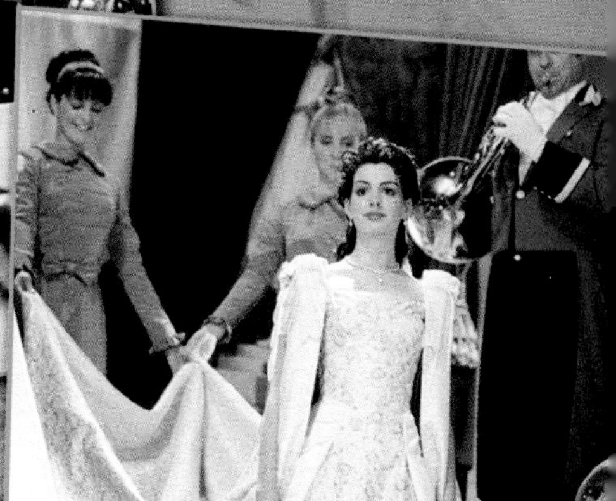

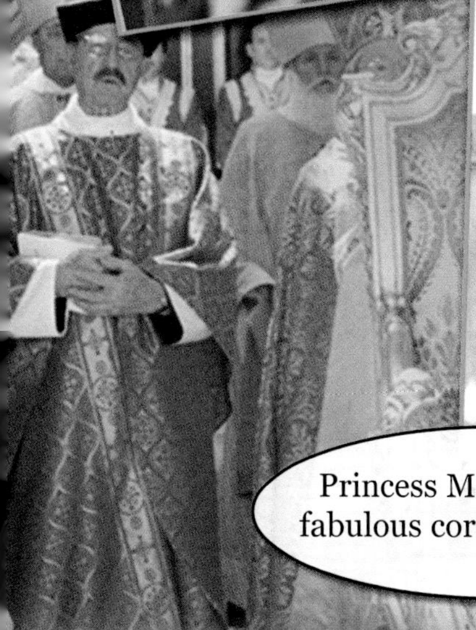

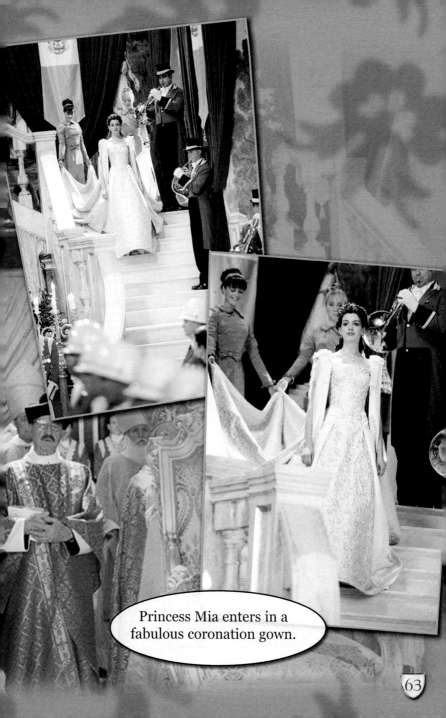

Princess Mia enters in a fabulous coronation gown.

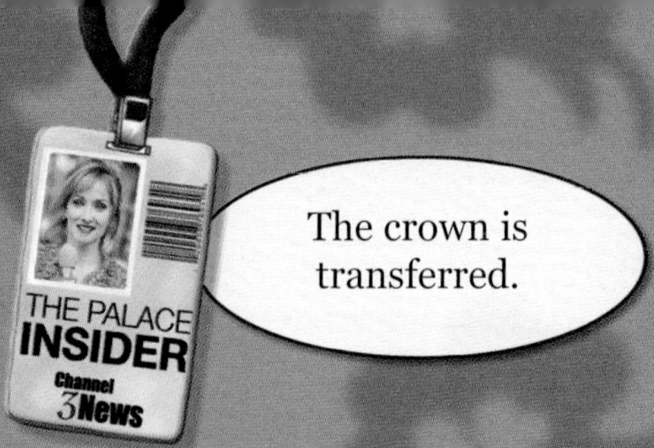
THE PALACE
INSIDER
Channel
3News
The crown is transferred.

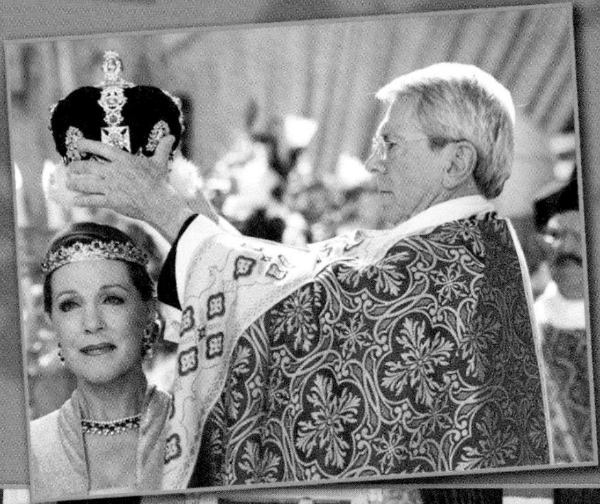

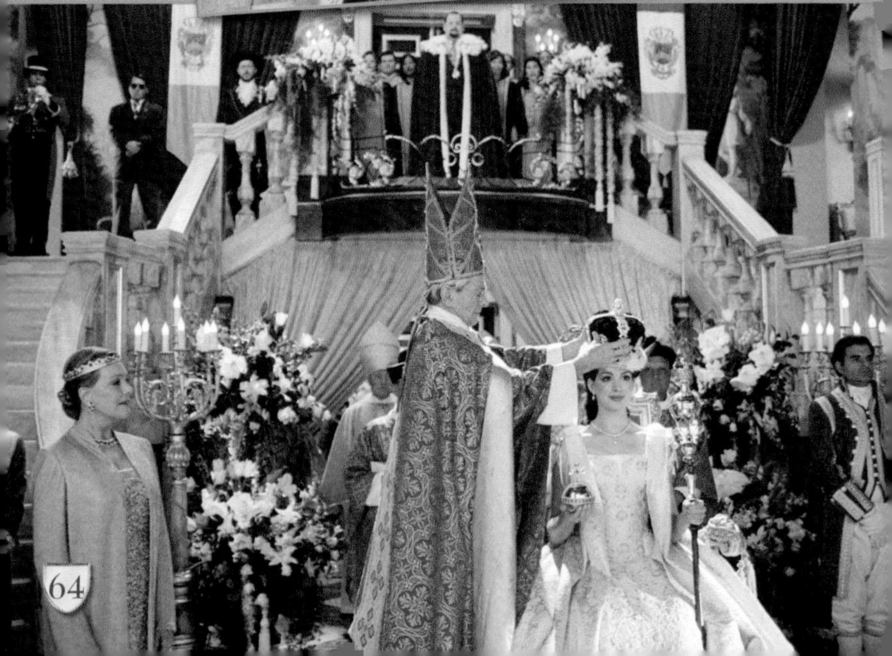

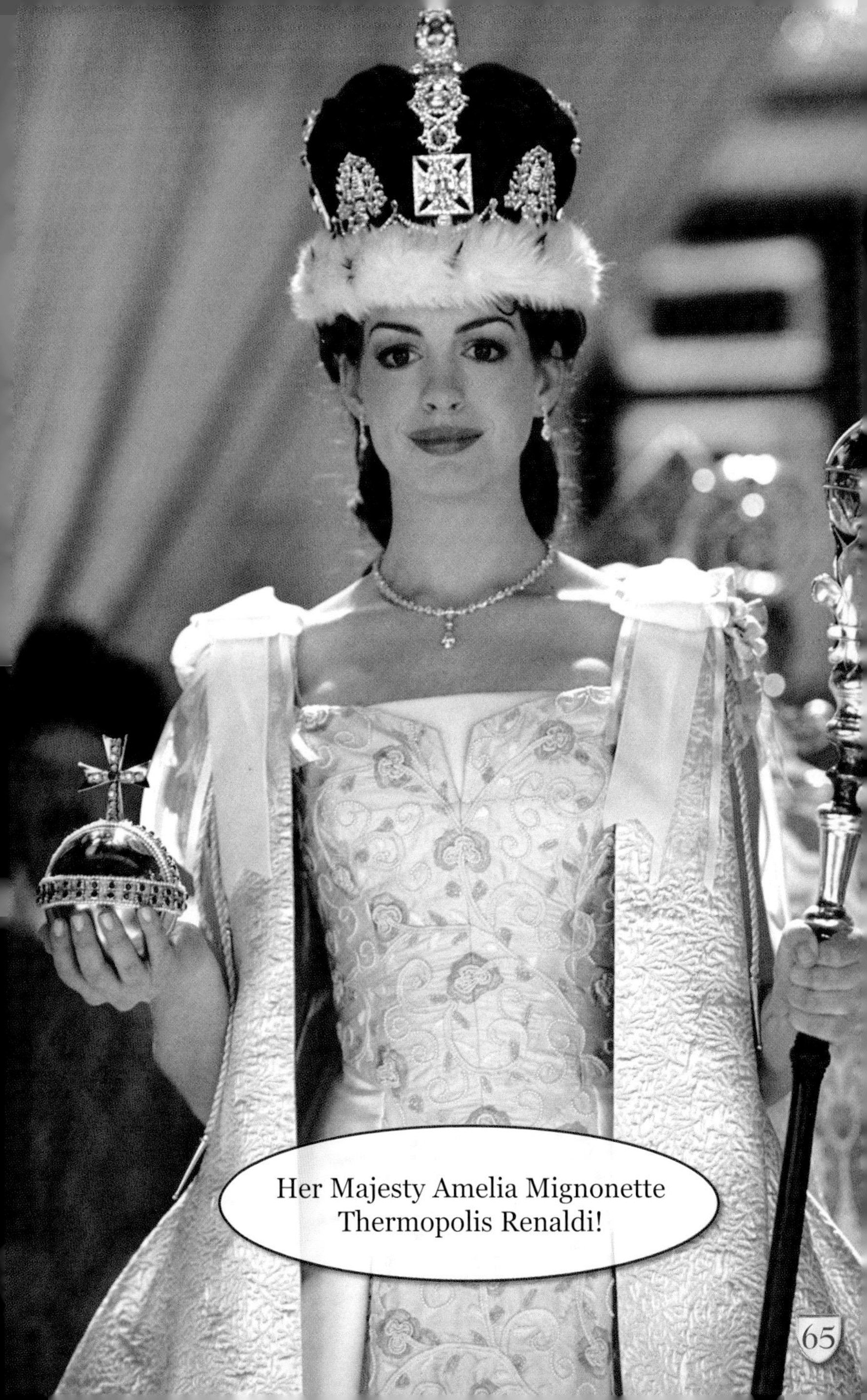
Her Majesty Amelia Mignonette Thermopolis Renaldi!

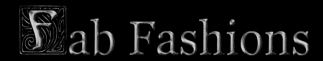

Fab Fashions

Princess Mia's royal wardrobe
is tiara-riffic!

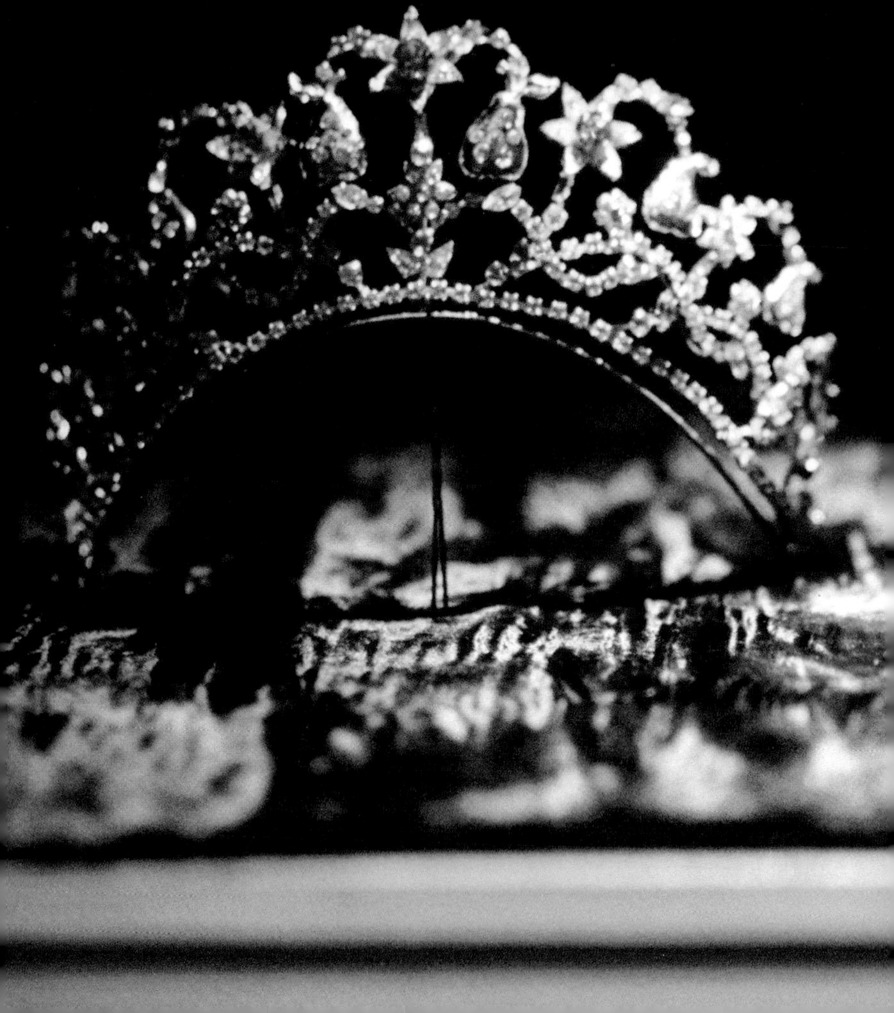

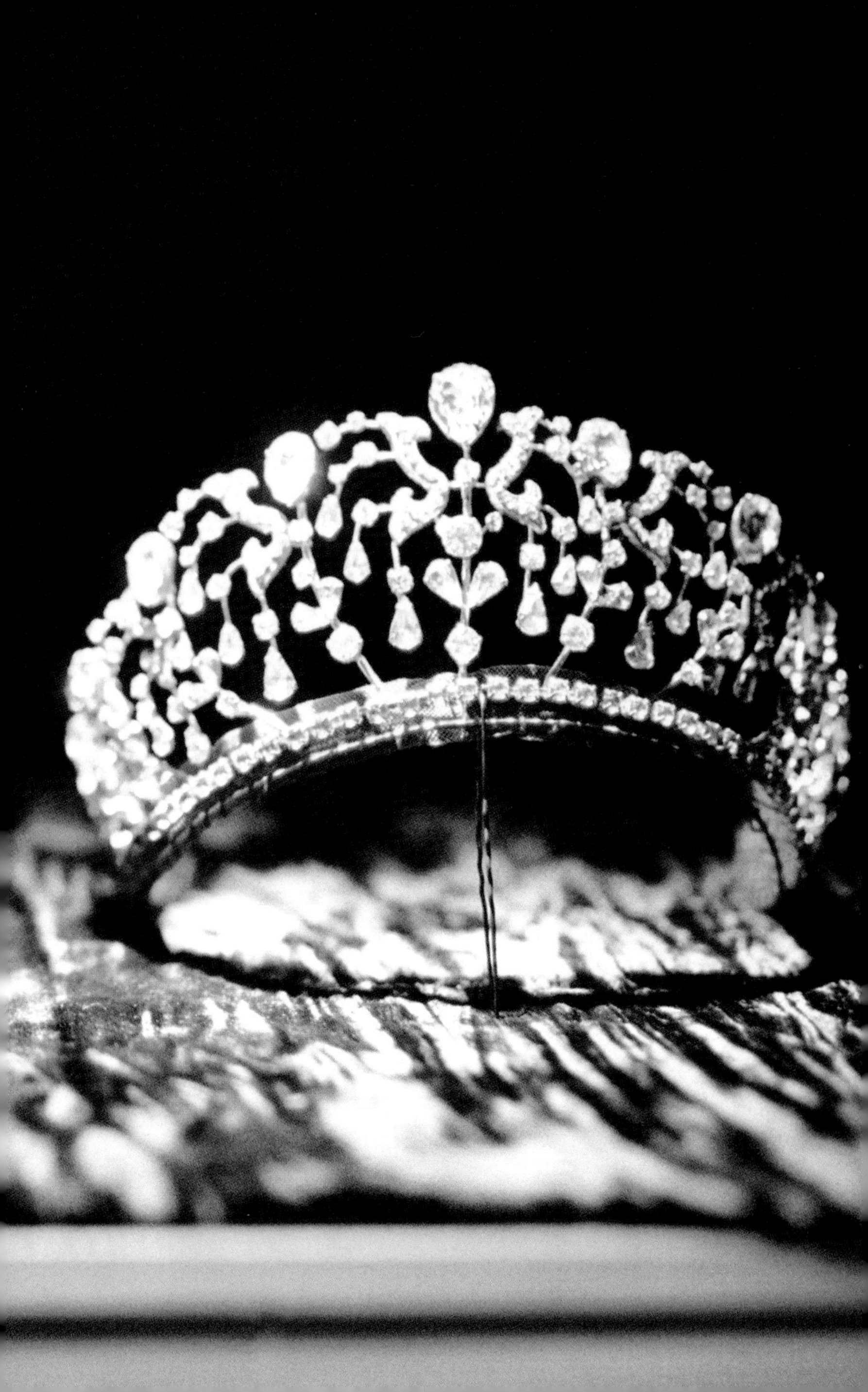

THE LADY IN RED AT HER BIRTHDAY BALL.

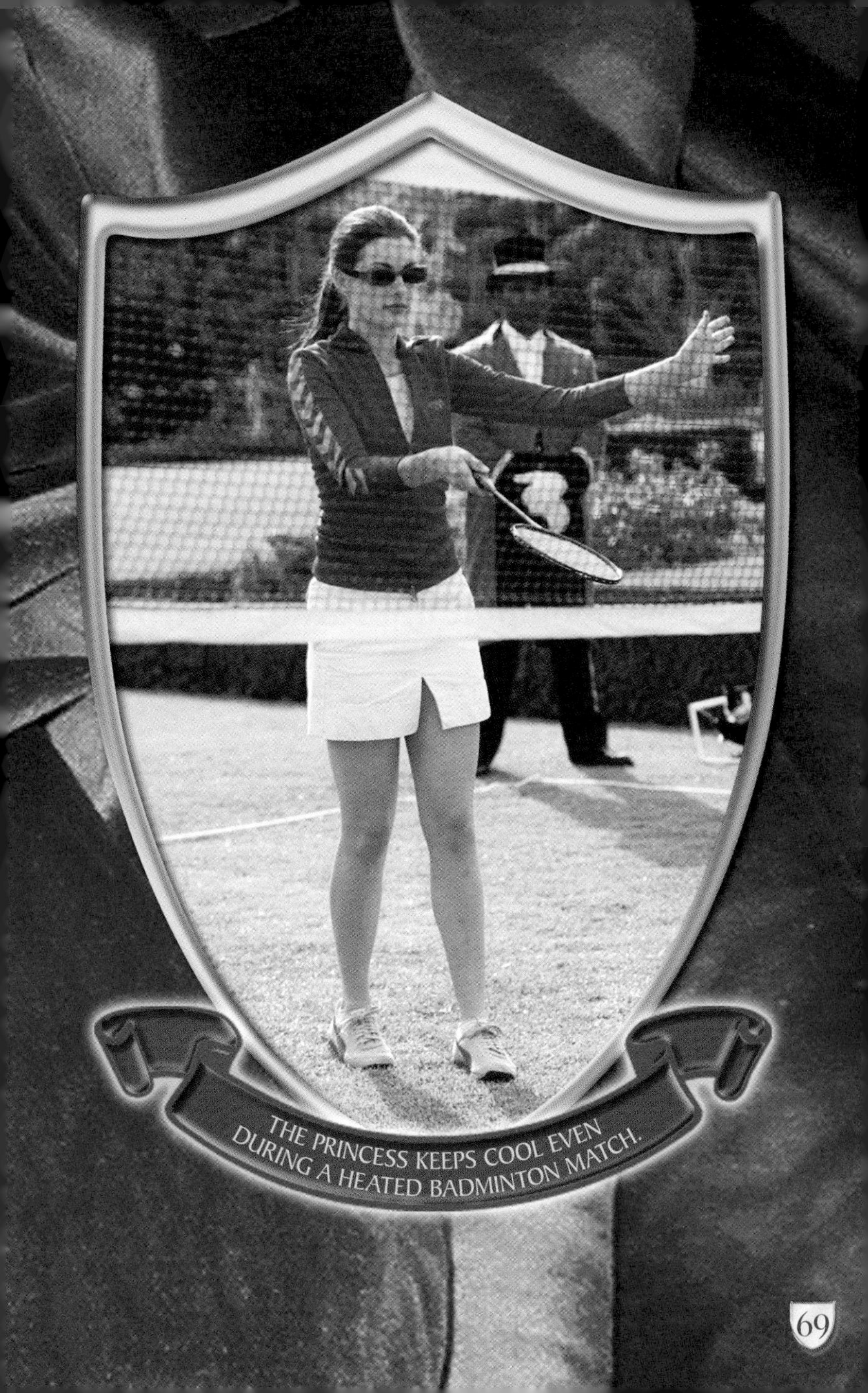

THE PRINCESS KEEPS COOL EVEN DURING A HEATED BADMINTON MATCH.

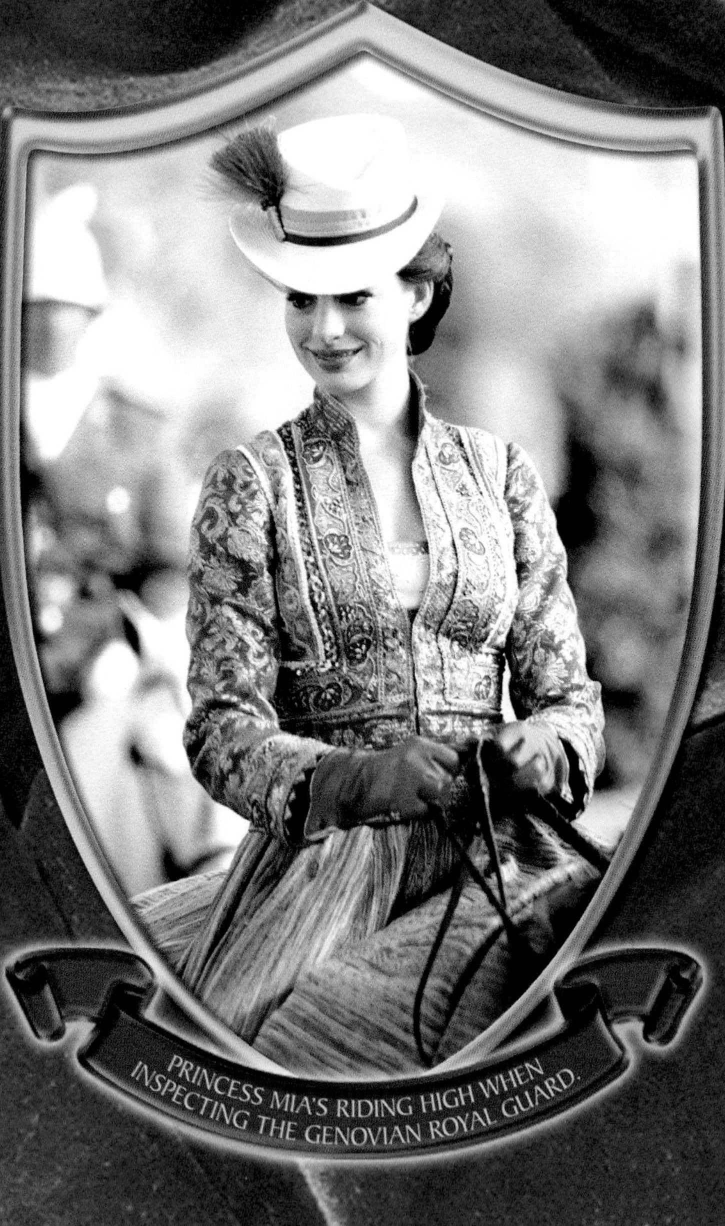

PRINCESS MIA'S RIDING HIGH WHEN INSPECTING THE GENOVIAN ROYAL GUARD.

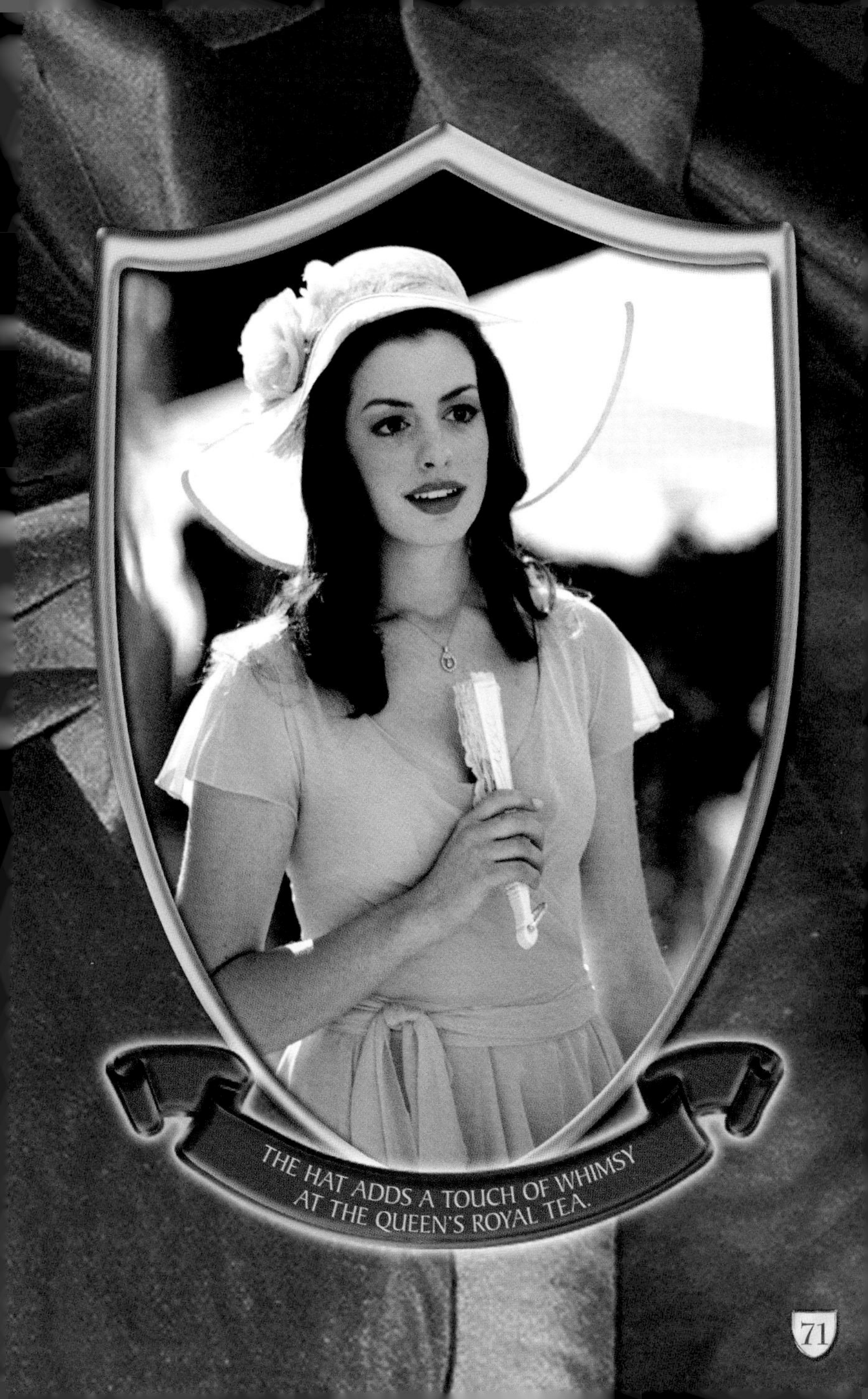

THE HAT ADDS A TOUCH OF WHIMSY
AT THE QUEEN'S ROYAL TEA.

FOR ARCHERY PRACTICE,
PRINCESS MIA DONS A SENSIBLE BLUE DRESS.

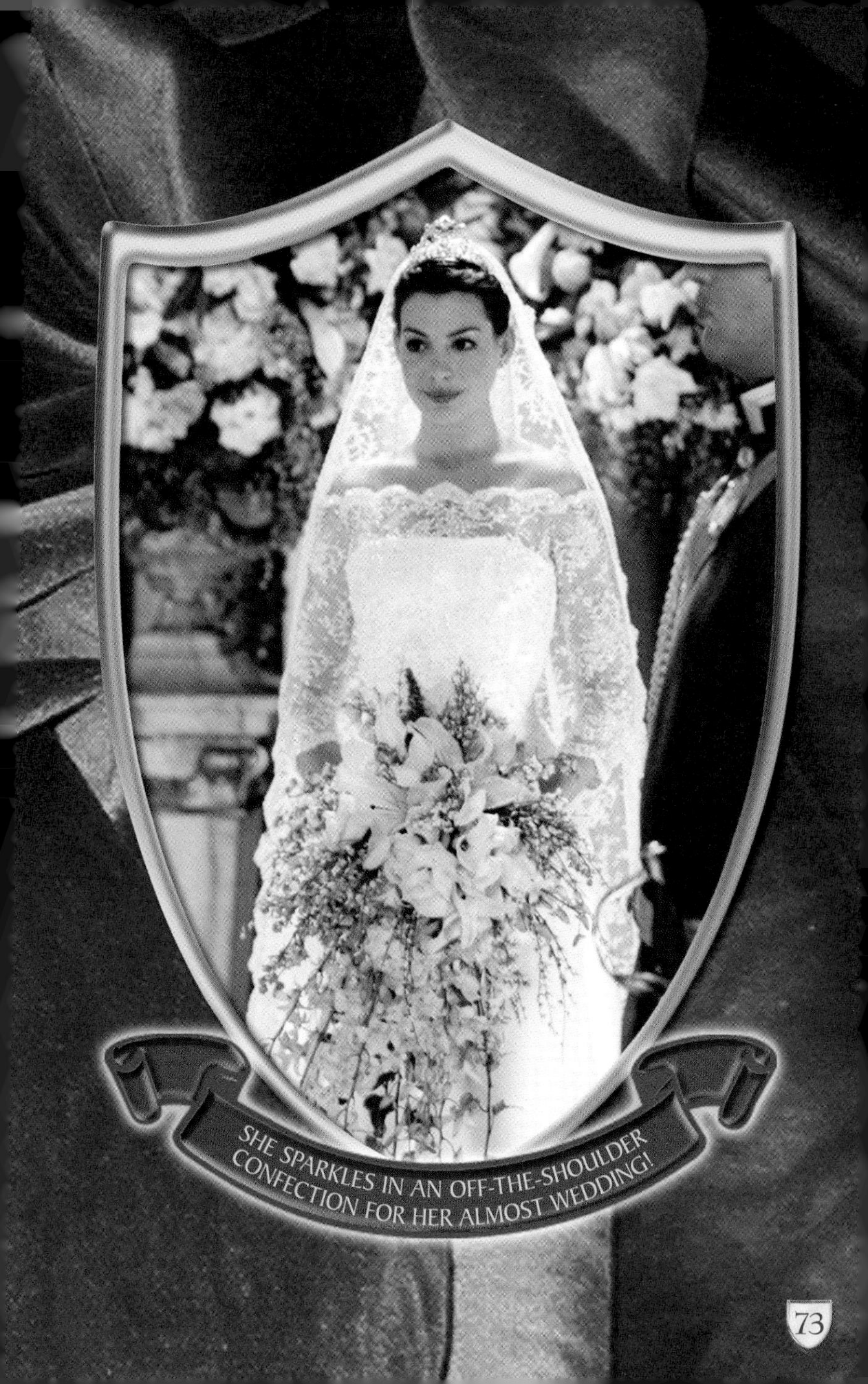

SHE SPARKLES IN AN OFF-THE-SHOULDER CONFECTION FOR HER ALMOST WEDDING!

THE CROWNING GLORY IS
THE NEW QUEEN'S CORONATION GOWN.

Bonus Boys!

More pics of Princess Mia's two men!

ANDREW!

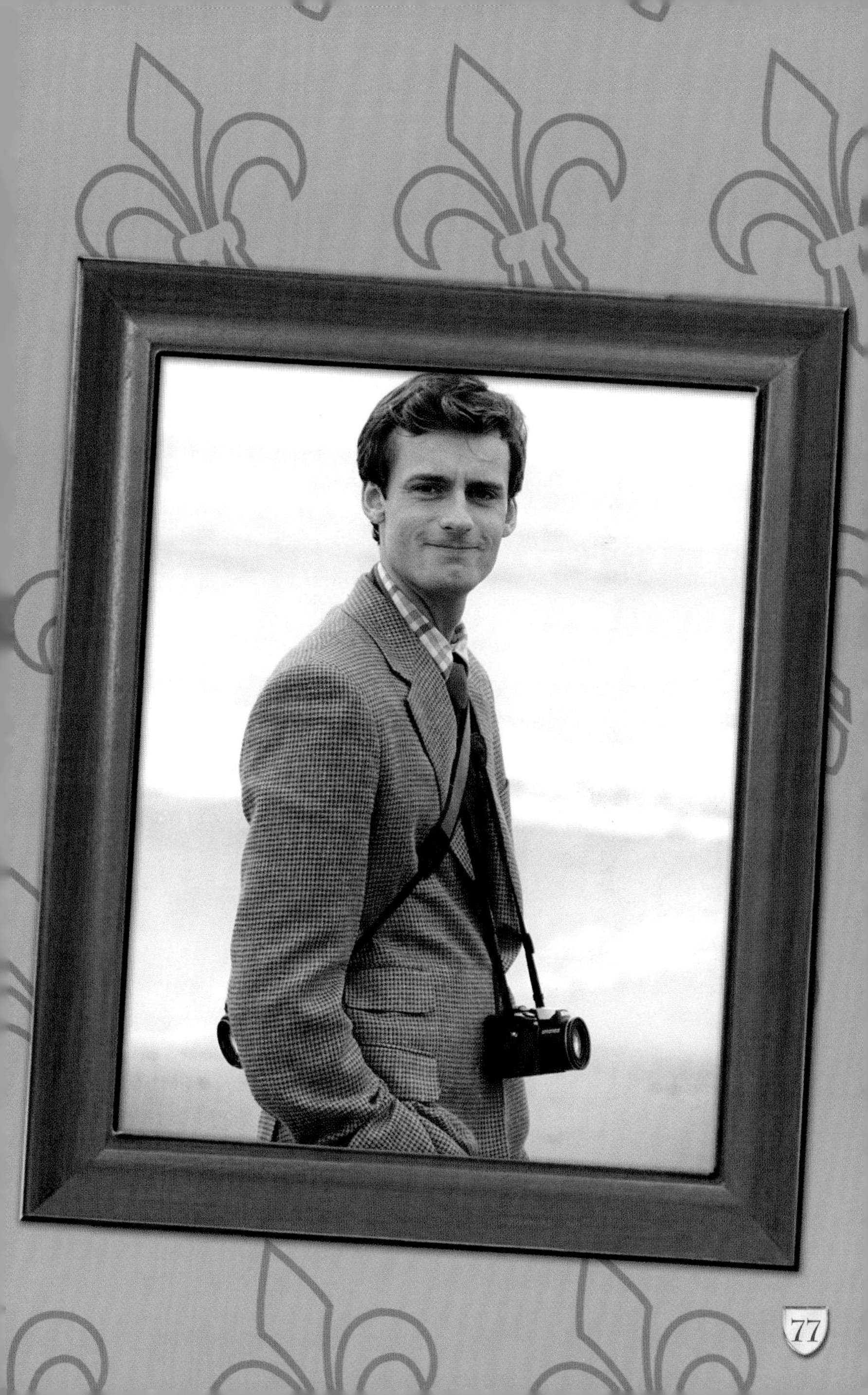

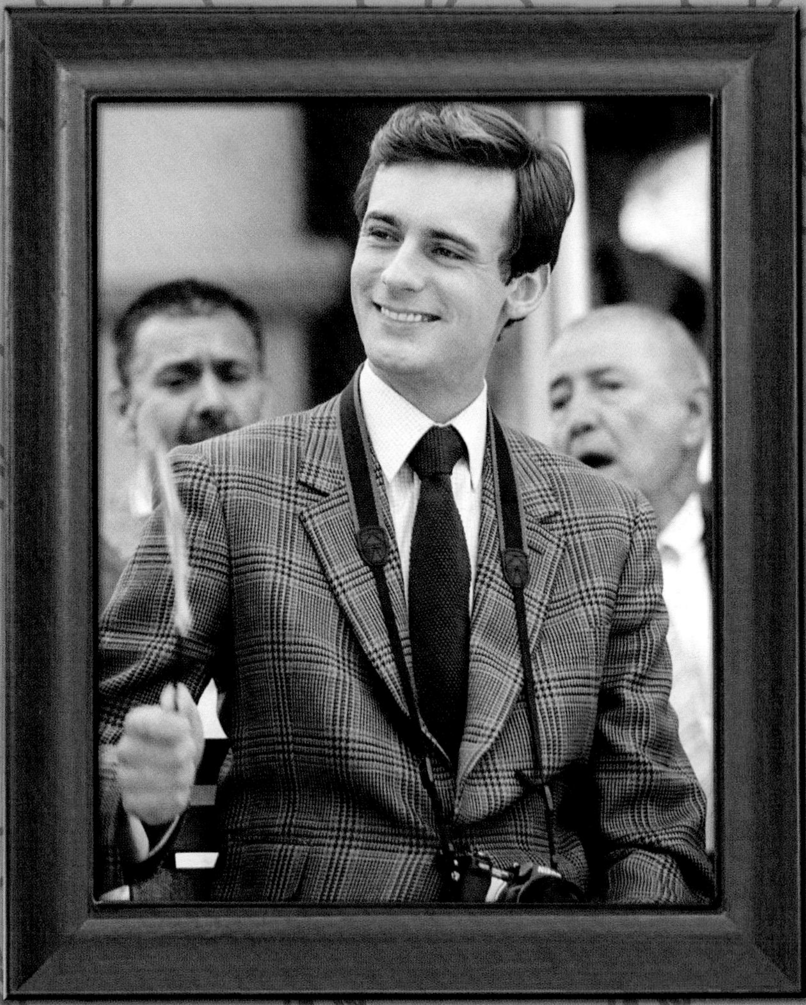

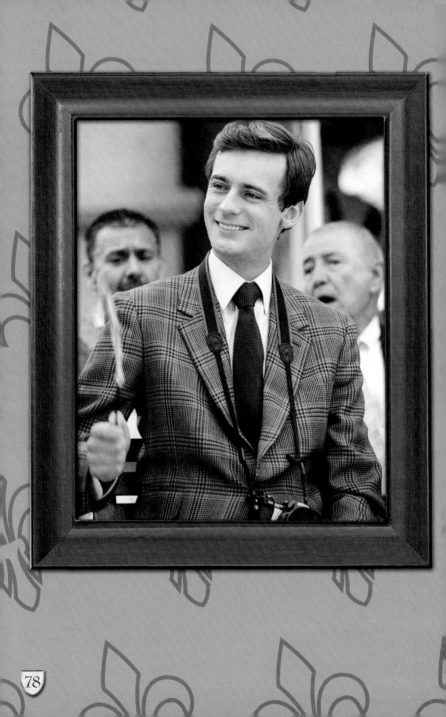

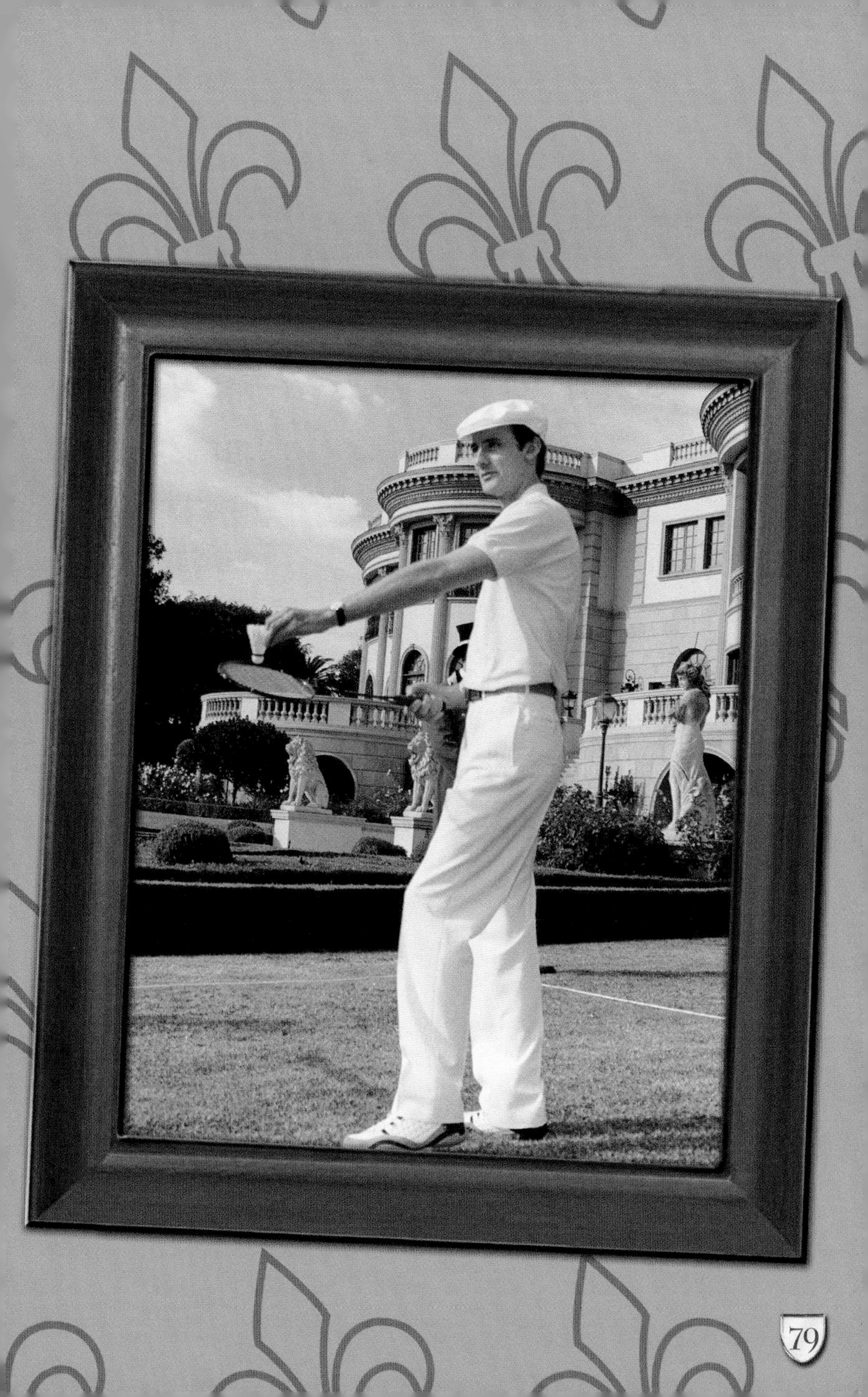

NICHOLAS!

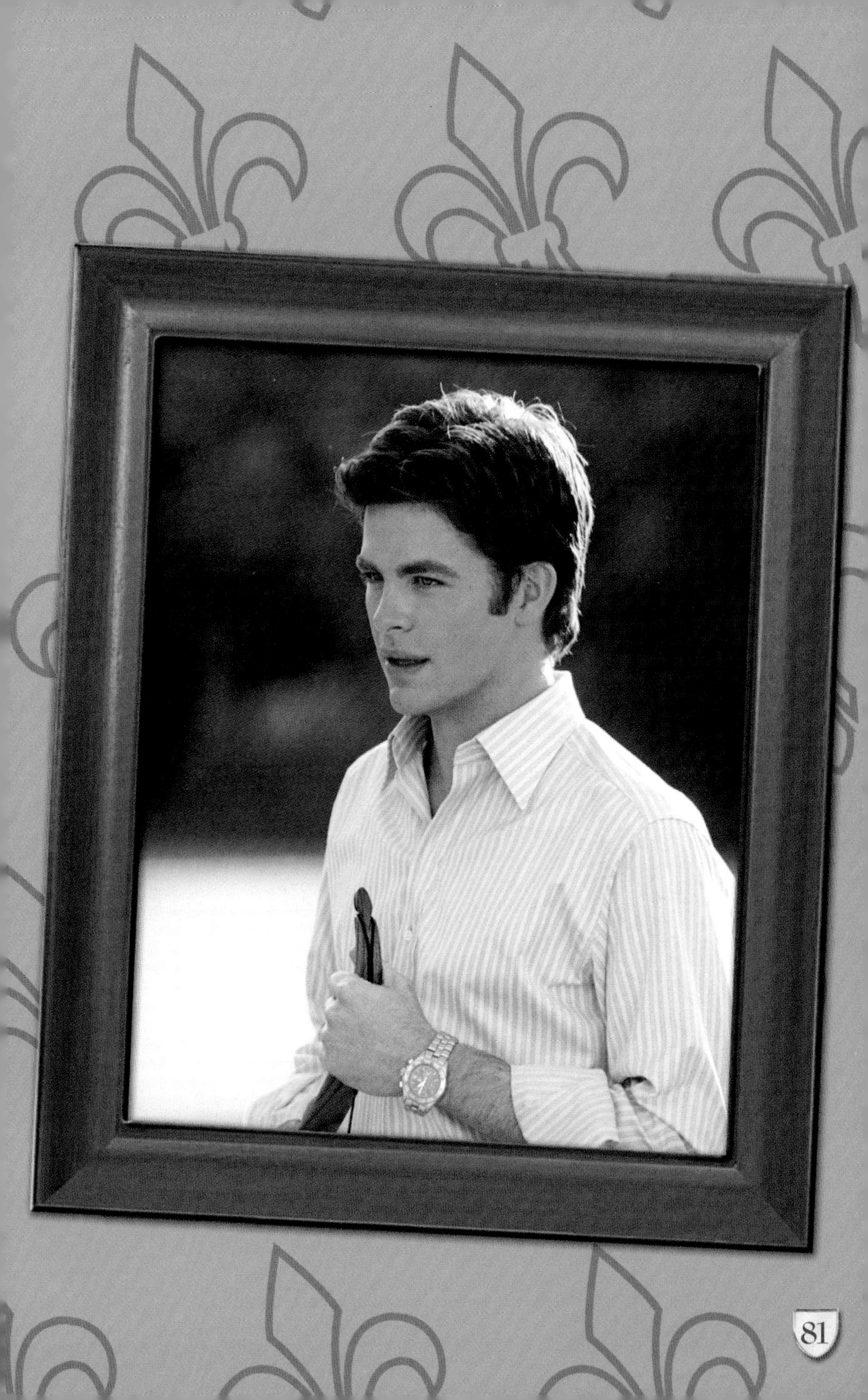

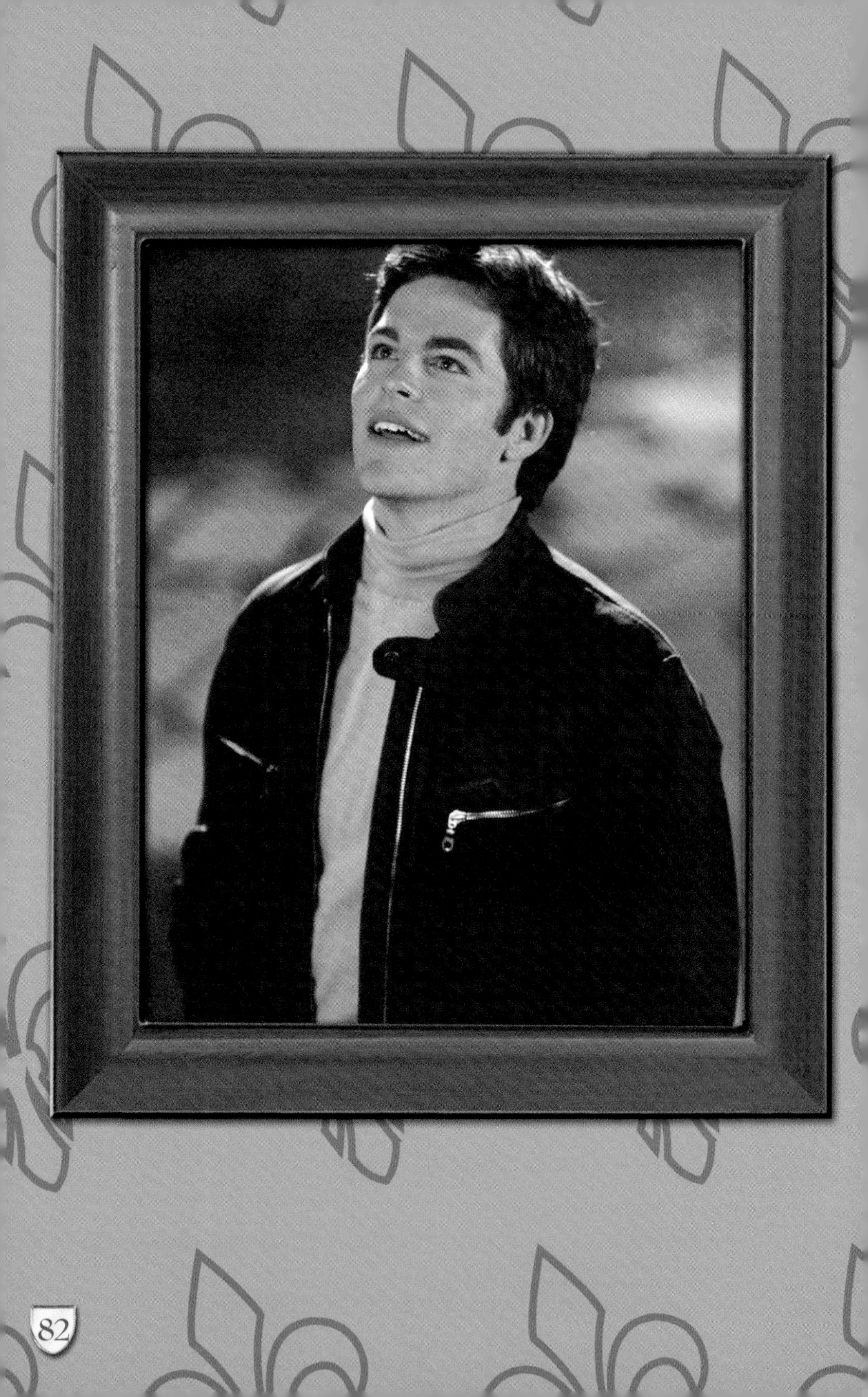

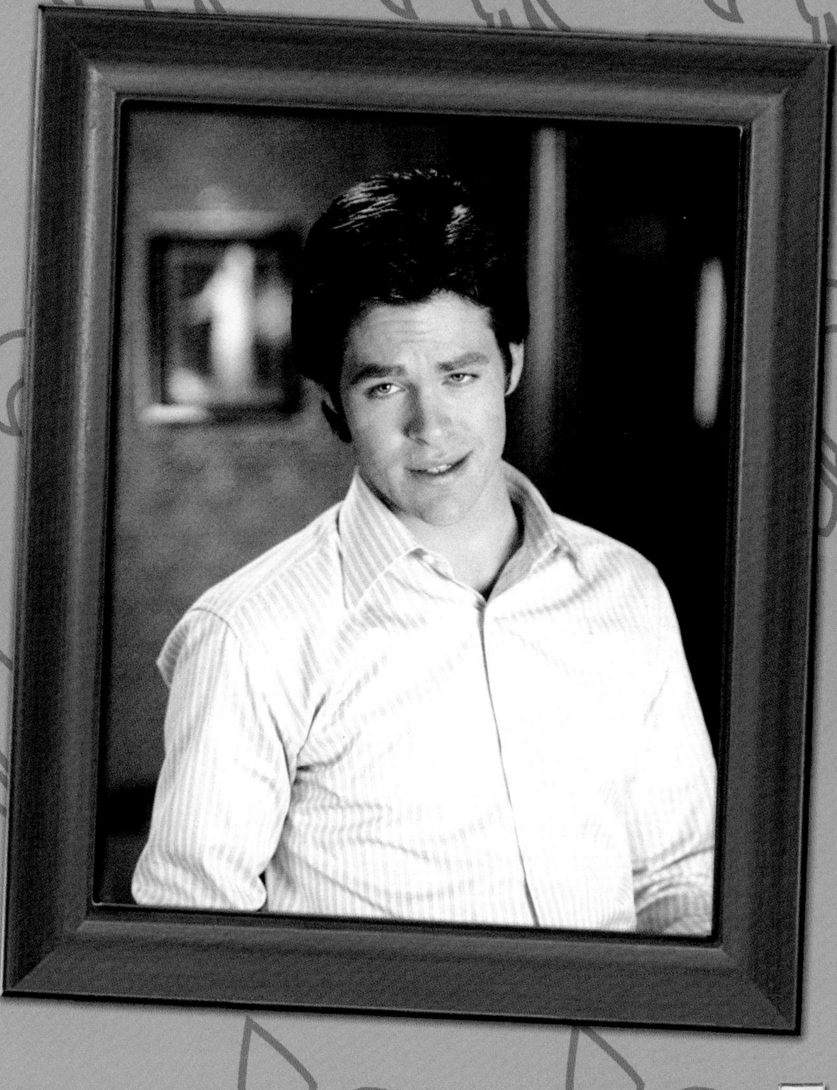

Behind the Scenes

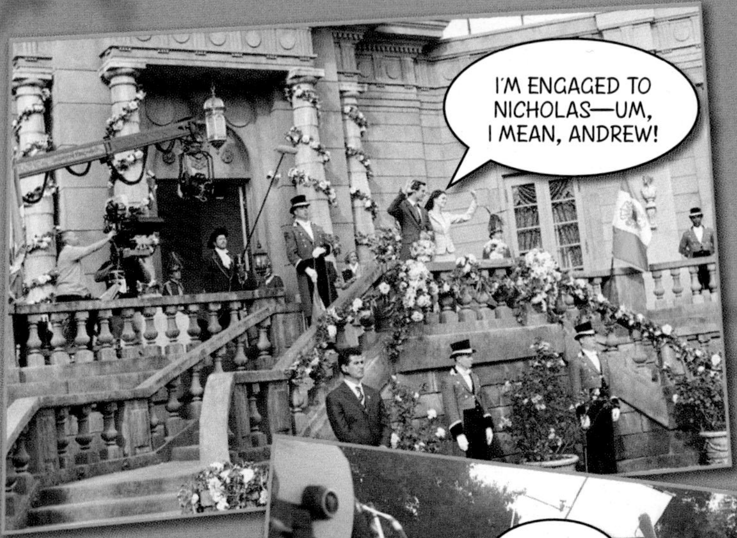
I'M ENGAGED TO NICHOLAS—UM, I MEAN, ANDREW!

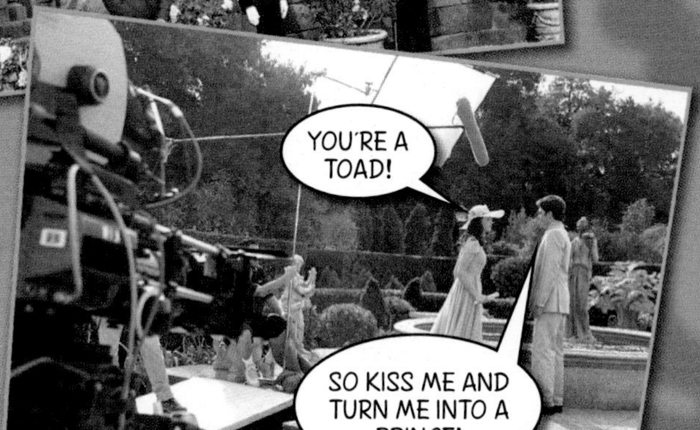
YOU'RE A TOAD!
SO KISS ME AND TURN ME INTO A PRINCE!

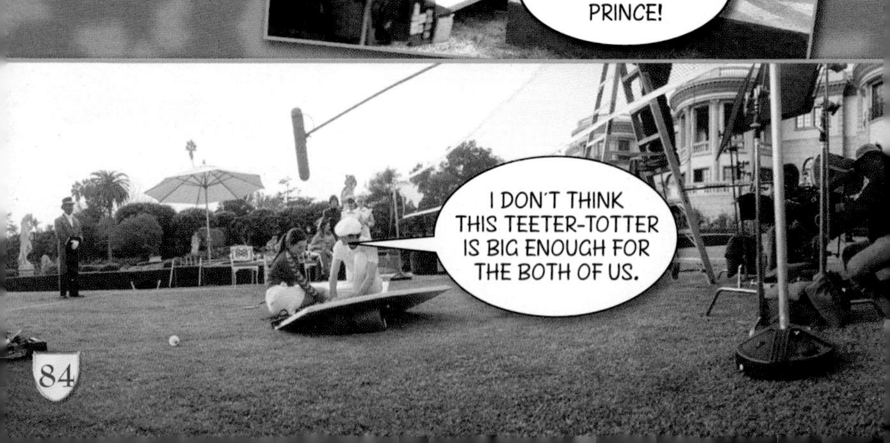
I DON'T THINK THIS TEETER-TOTTER IS BIG ENOUGH FOR THE BOTH OF US.

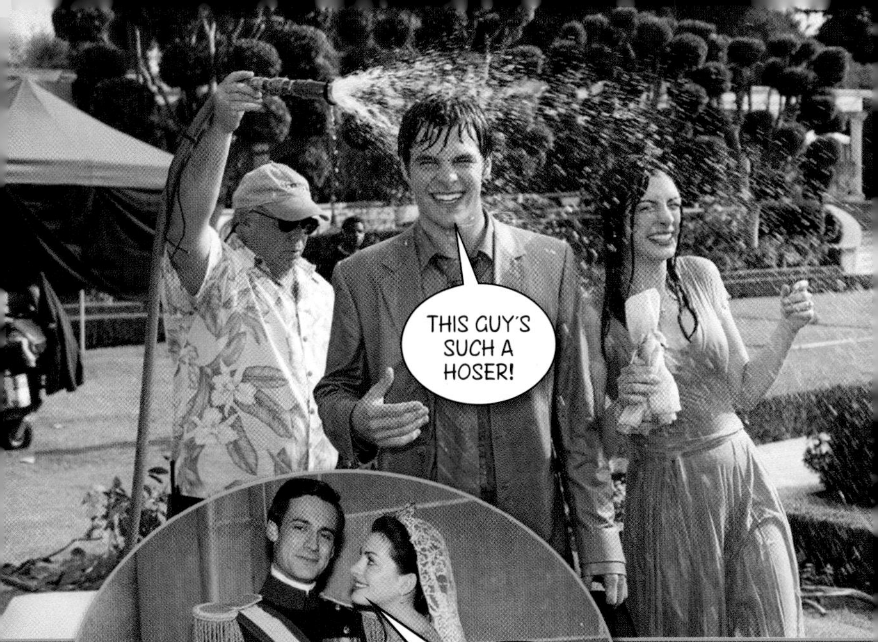
THIS GUY'S SUCH A HOSER!

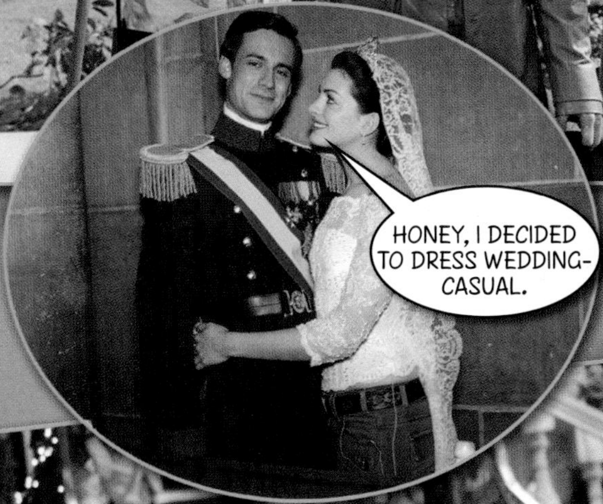
HONEY, I DECIDED TO DRESS WEDDING-CASUAL.

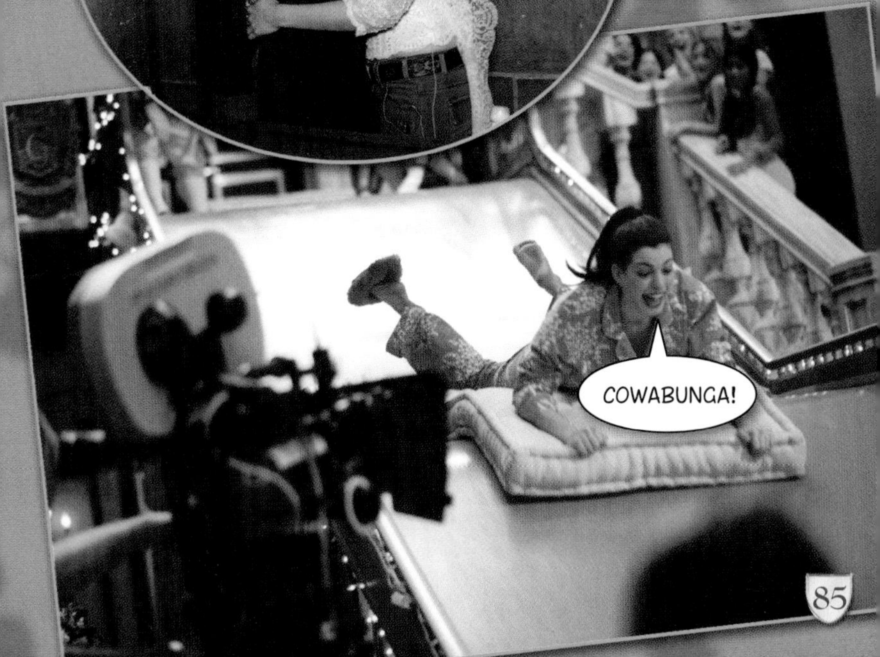
COWABUNGA!

ALSO AVAILABLE FROM ◎TOKYOPOP®

MANGA

.HACK//LEGEND OF THE TWILIGHT
ALICHINO
ANGELIC LAYER
BABY BIRTH
BRAIN POWERED
BRIGADOON
B'TX
CANDIDATE FOR GODDESS, THE
CARDCAPTOR SAKURA
CARDCAPTOR SAKURA - MASTER OF THE CLOW
CHRONICLES OF THE CURSED SWORD
CLAMP SCHOOL DETECTIVES
CLOVER
COMIC PARTY
CORRECTOR YUI
COWBOY BEBOP
COWBOY BEBOP: SHOOTING STAR
CRESCENT MOON
CROSS
CULDCEPT
CYBORG 009
D•N•ANGEL
DEARS
DEMON DIARY
DEMON ORORON, THE
DIGIMON
DIGIMON TAMERS
DIGIMON ZERO TWO
DRAGON HUNTER
DRAGON KNIGHTS
DRAGON VOICE
DREAM SAGA
DUKLYON: CLAMP SCHOOL DEFENDERS
ET CETERA
ETERNITY
FAERIES' LANDING
FLCL
FLOWER OF THE DEEP SLEEP, THE
FORBIDDEN DANCE
FRUITS BASKET
G GUNDAM
GATEKEEPERS
GIRL GOT GAME
GUNDAM SEED ASTRAY
GUNDAM WING
GUNDAM WING: BATTLEFIELD OF PACIFISTS
GUNDAM WING: ENDLESS WALTZ
GUNDAM WING: THE LAST OUTPOST (G-UNIT)
HANDS OFF!

HARLEM BEAT
HYPER RUNE
I.N.V.U.
INITIAL D
INSTANT TEEN: JUST ADD NUTS
JING: KING OF BANDITS
JING: KING OF BANDITS - TWILIGHT TALES
JULINE
KARE KANO
KILL ME, KISS ME
KINDAICHI CASE FILES, THE
KING OF HELL
KODOCHA: SANA'S STAGE
LEGEND OF CHUN HYANG, THE
LOVE OR MONEY
MAGIC KNIGHT RAYEARTH I
MAGIC KNIGHT RAYEARTH II
MAN OF MANY FACES
MARMALADE BOY
MARS
MARS: HORSE WITH NO NAME
MINK
MIRACLE GIRLS
MODEL
MOURYOU KIDEN: LEGEND OF THE NYMPHS
NECK AND NECK
ONE
ONE I LOVE, THE
PEACH GIRL
PEACH GIRL: CHANGE OF HEART
PITA-TEN
PLANET LADDER
PLANETES
PRESIDENT DAD
PRINCESS AI
PSYCHIC ACADEMY
QUEEN'S KNIGHT, THE
RAGNAROK
RAVE MASTER
REALITY CHECK
REBIRTH
REBOUND
RISING STARS OF MANGA
SAILOR MOON
SAINT TAIL
SAMURAI GIRL REAL BOUT HIGH SCHOOL
SEIKAI TRILOGY, THE
SGT. FROG
SHAOLIN SISTERS
SHIRAHIME-SYO: SNOW GODDESS TALES

08.20.04Y

ALSO AVAILABLE FROM  TOKYOPOP®

08.20.04Y

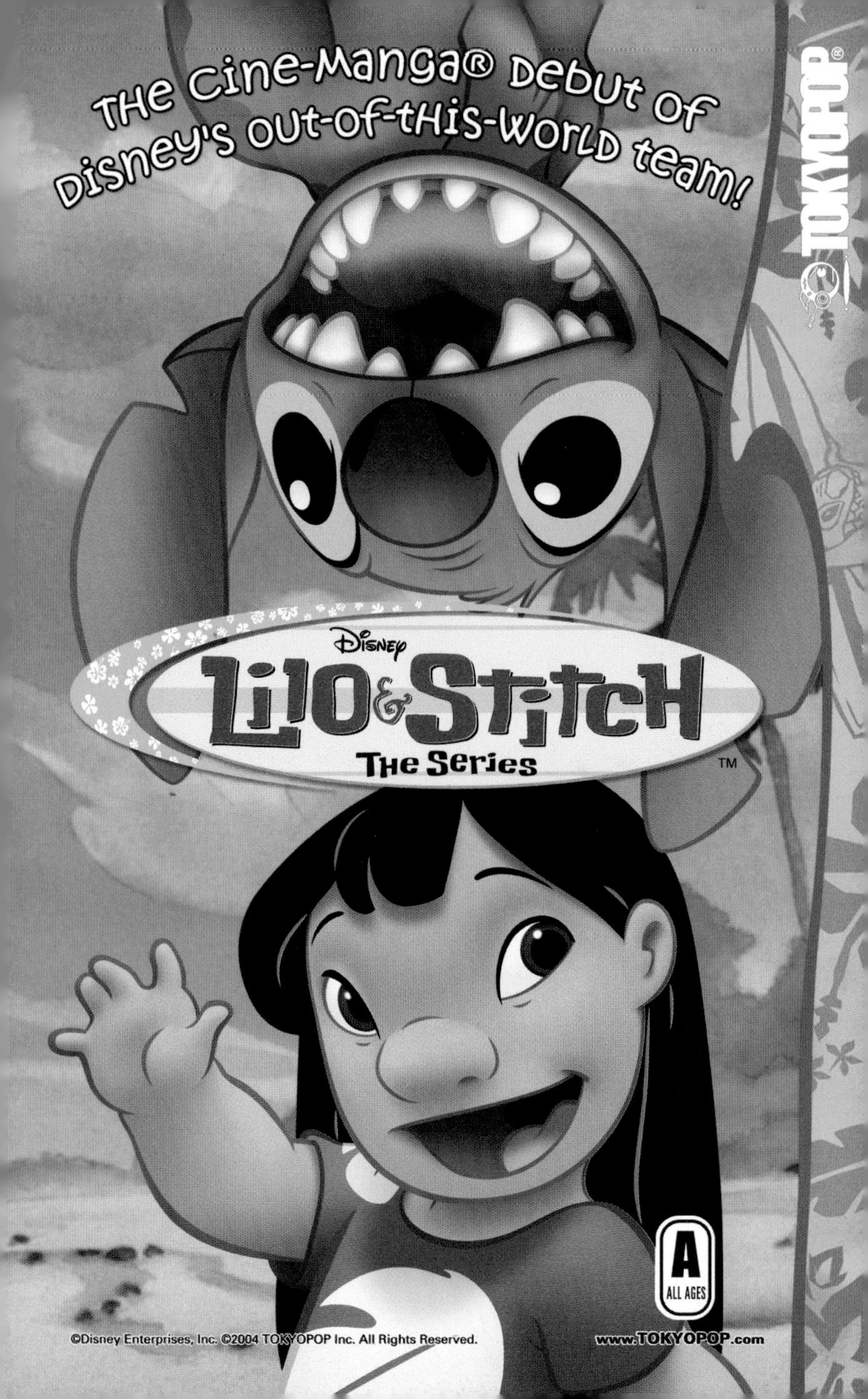

THE Cine-Manga® DeBut of Disney's out-of-this-world team!
TOKYOPOP®
Disney
Lilo & Stitch The Series ™
A ALL AGES

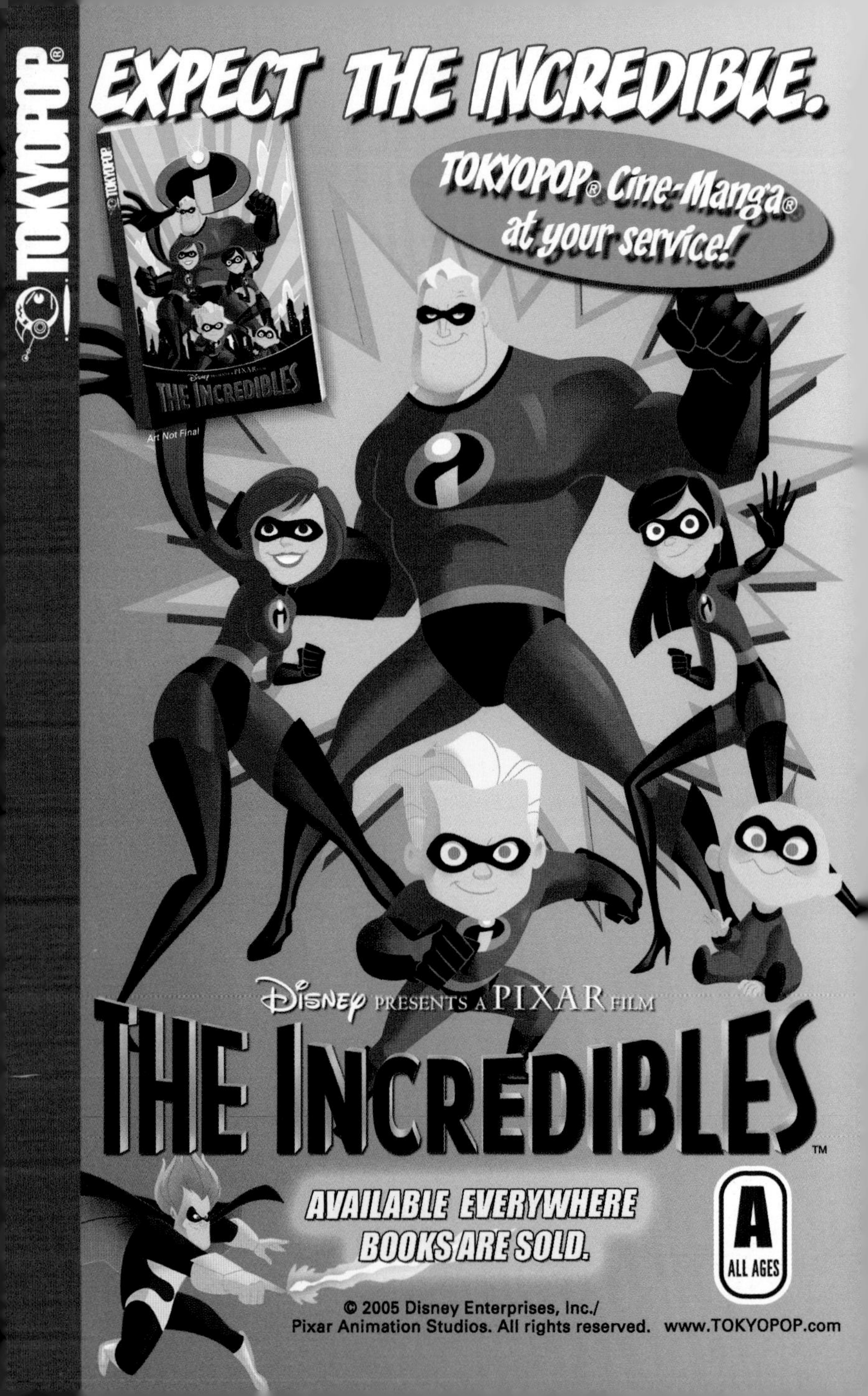
TOKYOPOP®
EXPECT THE INCREDIBLE.
TOKYOPOP® Cine-Manga®
at your service!
THE INCREDIBLES
Art Not Final
DISNEY PRESENTS A PIXAR FILM
THE INCREDIBLES™
AVAILABLE EVERYWHERE
BOOKS ARE SOLD.
A
ALL AGES
© 2005 Disney Enterprises, Inc./
Pixar Animation Studios. All rights reserved.
www.TOKYOPOP.com

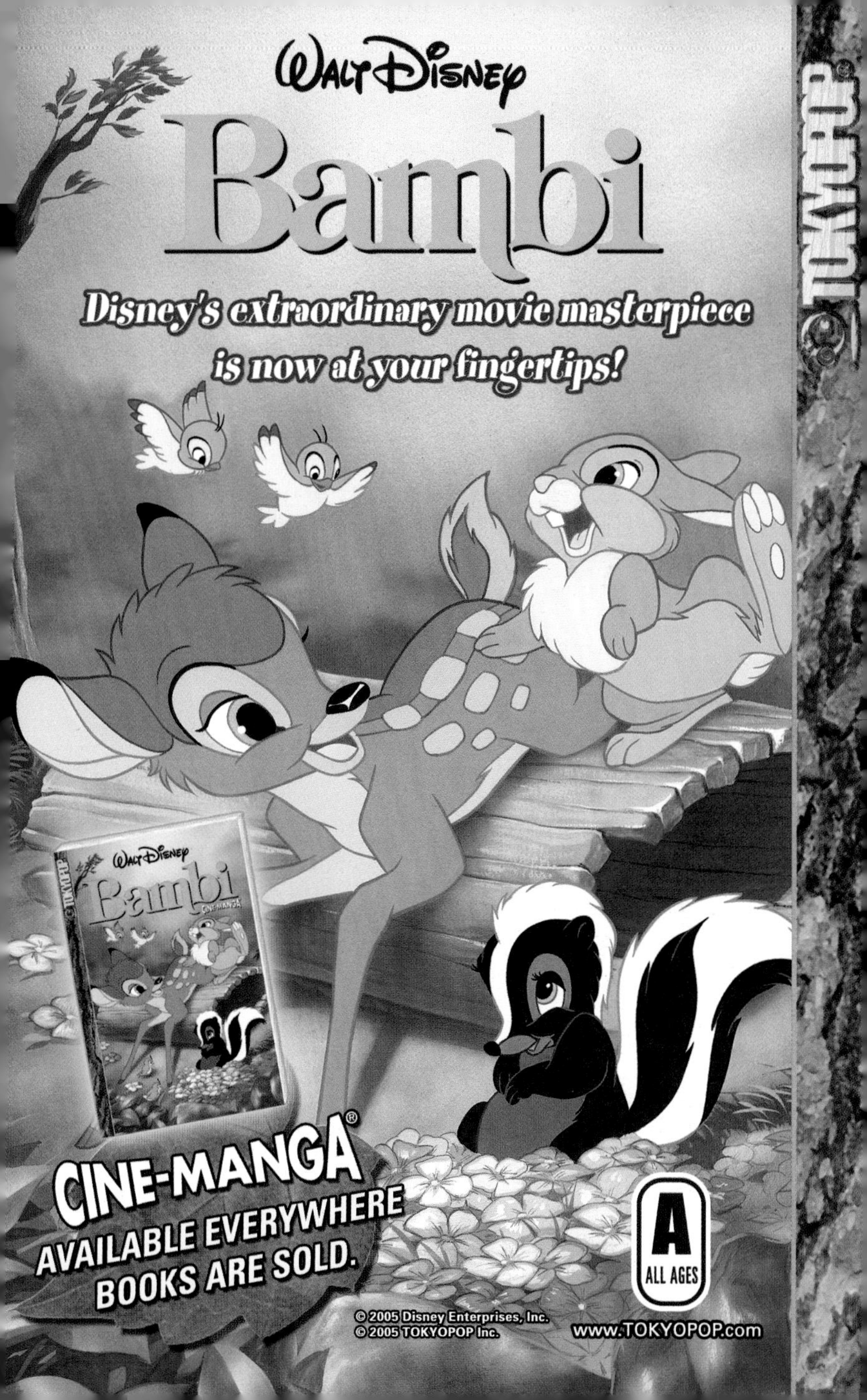
Walt Disney
Bambi
Disney's extraordinary movie masterpiece
is now at your fingertips!
CINE-MANGA®
AVAILABLE EVERYWHERE
BOOKS ARE SOLD.
A
ALL AGES
© 2005 Disney Enterprises, Inc.
© 2005 TOKYOPOP Inc.
www.TOKYOPOP.com
TOKYOPOP

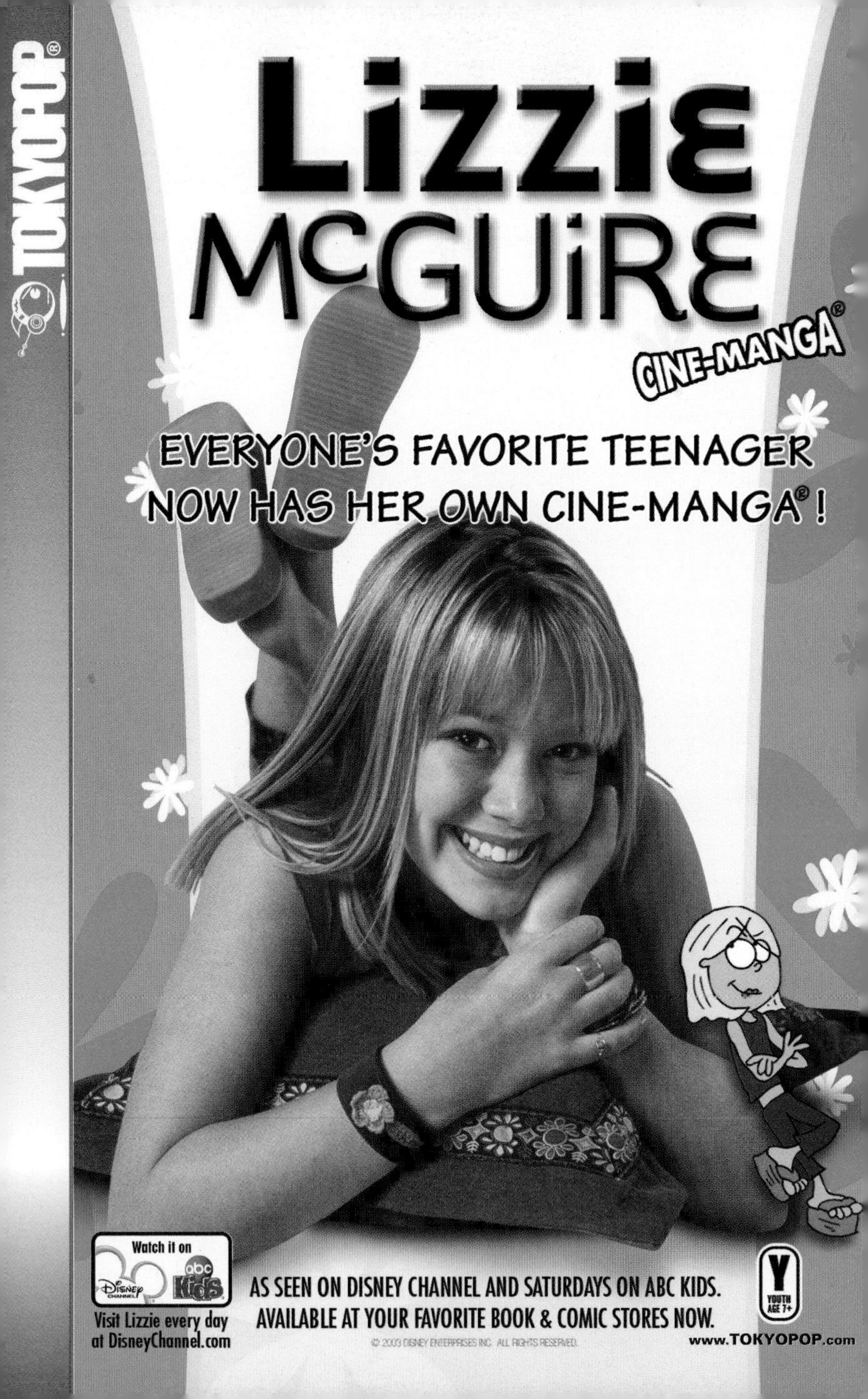
TOKYOPOP
Lizzie McGUIRE
CINE-MANGA®
EVERYONE'S FAVORITE TEENAGER
NOW HAS HER OWN CINE-MANGA®!
Watch it on
Disney Channel
abc Kids
Visit Lizzie every day at DisneyChannel.com
AS SEEN ON DISNEY CHANNEL AND SATURDAYS ON ABC KIDS.
AVAILABLE AT YOUR FAVORITE BOOK & COMIC STORES NOW.
© 2003 DISNEY ENTERPRISES INC. ALL RIGHTS RESERVED.
Y
YOUTH AGE 7+
www.TOKYOPOP.com

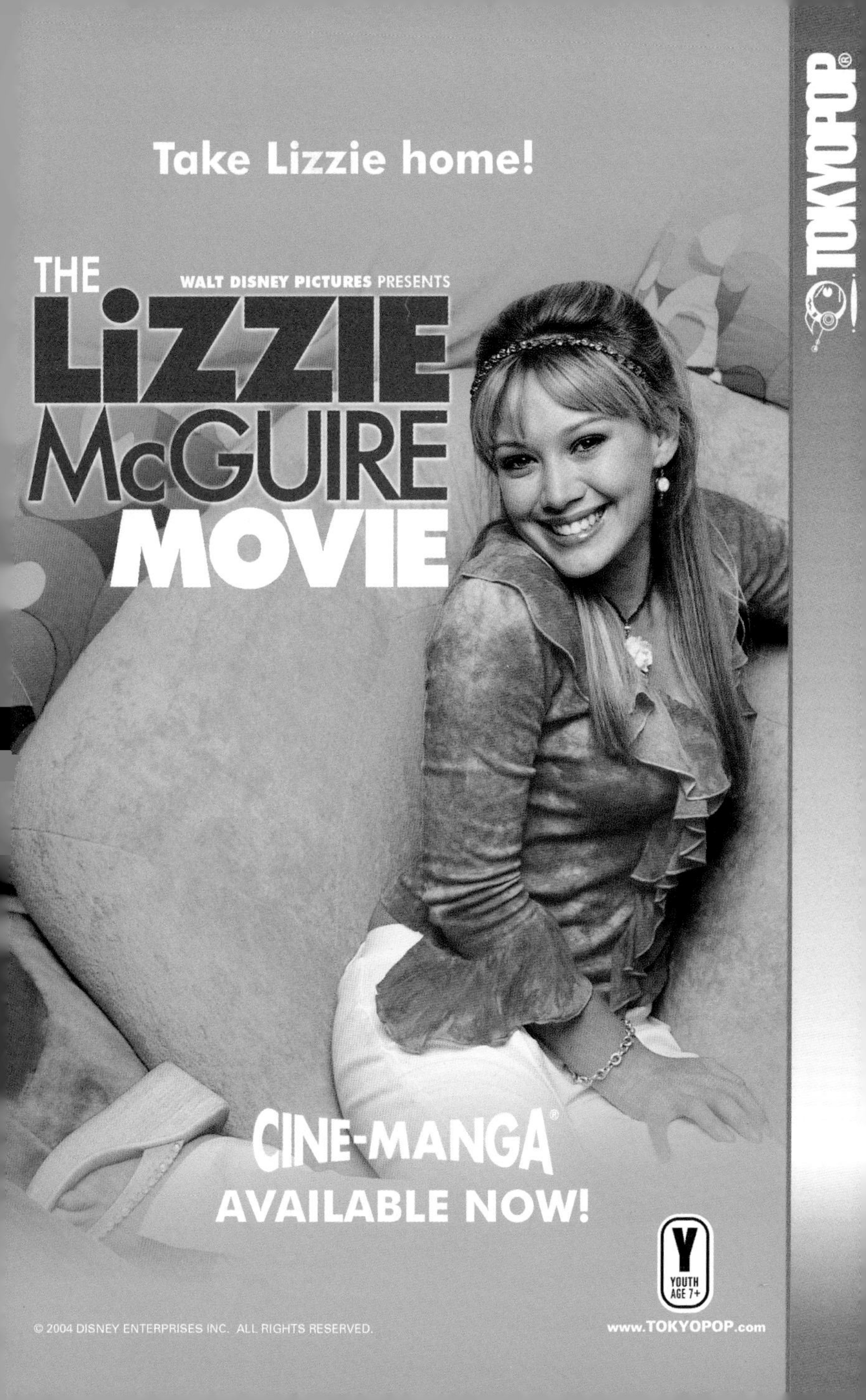

Take Lizzie home!

WALT DISNEY PICTURES PRESENTS

THE LiZZiE McGUIRE MOVIE

CINE-MANGA®
AVAILABLE NOW!

www.**TOKYOPOP**.com

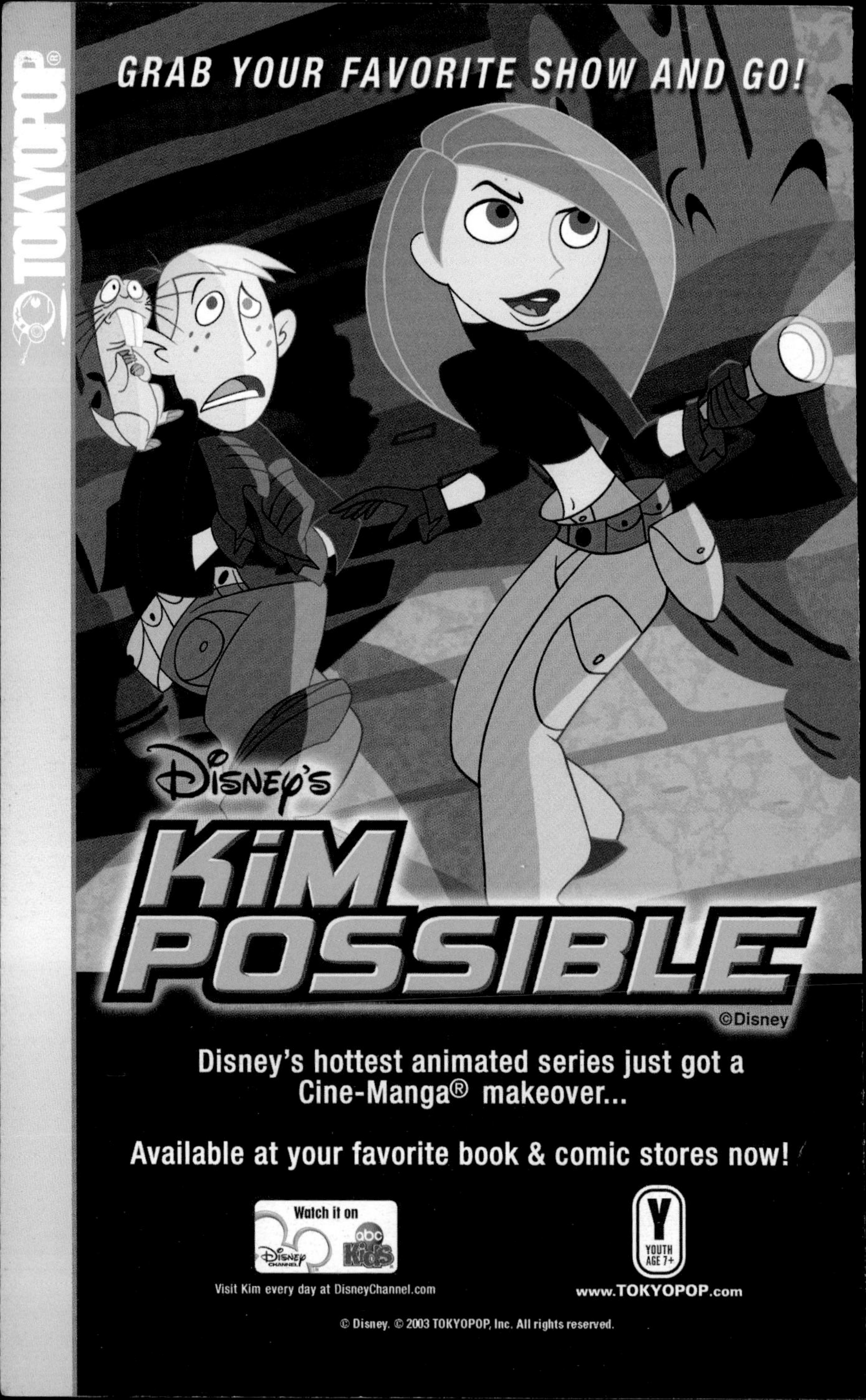
TOKYOPOP
GRAB YOUR FAVORITE SHOW AND GO!
Disney's
KiM POSSIBLE
©Disney
Disney's hottest animated series just got a Cine-Manga® makeover...
Available at your favorite book & comic stores now!
Watch it on
Disney Channel
abc Kids
Visit Kim every day at DisneyChannel.com
Y
YOUTH AGE 7+
www.TOKYOPOP.com
© Disney. © 2003 TOKYOPOP, Inc. All rights reserved.